IVY DREAMS

IVY DREAMS

Jill Eisnaugle

Ivy Dreams

This book is a work of fiction. Any names, characters or incidents are either products of the author's imagination or are used fictitiously. Any resemblance to actual events or persons, living or dead, is entirely coincidental.

ISBN 978-0-578-11353-1

Dedication

For Roger, Heather, and their children

May the beauty of baseball remain in your souls
for as long as your love remains in your hearts!

"When the final strike is rendered
and another season's through,
Baseball's joys shall be remembered
in the calls, splendid and true."

Acknowledgments

Thank you, Dad, for instilling the love for baseball and respect for broadcasting in my heart.

Thanks, Mom, for tolerating the years of friendly sports debates and the countless baseball and broadcasting stories that Dad and I rehashed so many times. I know you'd heard the stories enough to recite them and yet, you never said a word when you heard them all again. It is because of the love and support you both showed me that I live my own dreams today.

With utmost respect and appreciation, thank you to Mary Lee Palmer for her tremendous support in the final weeks of writing *Ivy Dreams*. You're such a rock of wisdom and encouragement in my life and there are no words for how many times you saved my sanity as I penned those last six chapters. You've definitely shown me that playing hardball every now and again is worth it.

Minister Lynn Turner, I appreciate how supportive of my writing passion you have always been and I'm grateful for the prayers you've extended along this journey, sometimes filled with curveballs I had to dodge.

To everyone back in Jackson County, Ohio, that respected and supported me while I grew up in rural America, I am grateful for your love and admiration, then and still. Special thanks to Regina Chaney, Sharon Needham, and newspaper editor Pete Wilson. My memory of leaving Jackson on a Greyhound bus, at the age of seven, to watch my first live Major League game has never left my heart.

Thanks to John Murray, III and Linda Franklin for their wisdom, advice, and expertise in making this novel so special. Your passions for writing and baseball made for great enthusiasm throughout the review and editing process.

Last, but not least, thank you to late Cubs broadcasters Ron Santo, Harry Caray, and Jack Brickhouse for making each and every Cub game exciting for the fans that tuned into the radio and television broadcasts. You kept it real and made each game beautiful, even when the Cubs were down by nine runs.

Foreword

Every spring, by the millions, baseball fans flock from their homes along the rural routes and metro loops of this great nation for one common objective: to follow a dream, lived however vicariously, through their undying love and support for their team. Yes, their team. The one team whose colors have run as purely as blood through their veins from the time that their fathers first loaded them into the family sedan, as children, so they could experience one day in the sun. A day spent in the bleachers basking in the glory of what nature has to offer, all for the sake of experiencing something far greater than anything else they would witness, prior to their eighteenth birthday (or, quite possibly, ever again in their lives). The days, and those trips to the ballpark, are priceless. From the time that first trip to the ballgame arrives, the memory becomes a father's ultimate gift to his child. It is a gift, packaged in the form of one special moment when father and child wholeheartedly experience fresh air and freedom, bonding and baseball. The beauty within that moment passes from generation to generation, eventually forming a family tradition, begun in part because of a father's love for his child and the game of baseball. It is the ultimate love – a love spanning days, months, years, decades and centuries, existing truer than the most timeless of romantic poems.

The truest fan of America's Pastime will thrive from that first baseball outing and grow to see a ground-rule double in his sleep, to smell the freshly cut grass in his nose, to taste the joy of victory upon his lips, to hear the cheers and boos from the crowd – as echoed upon the wind – and to feel the aura in all of those things, regardless of the date on the calendar.

The baseball enthusiast will pride himself on the great calls of the game as he attempts, however unsuccessfully, to imitate the "Hey-Heys," "Holy Cows," and "She i-i-i-is gones" that had been uttered by the spectacular broadcasting legends of our time. He will stay up late, through thick and thin, following the calls on television or radio – if not witnessed in person – only to turn around the next day and do it again. The fan's persistence is the direct result of his passion for the team, the pursuance of a dream, and the personal admiration that comes from witnessing a simple game of balls and strikes.

Factory employees, iron workers, office staff, food service personnel, and everyone from company vice presidents to administrative professionals and you are one and the same for six months of each calendar year. Joined by a shared interest in the sport and united by a common thread – a love for the game – each fan harbors the same desire: the power of a dream. It does not matter if that dream is to watch their favorite player hit a home run or to witness a rookie batter stretch his first Major League double into a triple. The dream that is Major League Baseball does not come from what happens in the present. For the everyday working man, the "dream" is being able to relive a small piece of one's past, if even for the shortest of moments, through the sights and sounds portrayed by those who manage, play, or call the game.

This story is about one baseball player's dream and her ability to make it happen; yet, while the scene depicted in this novel occurred on the baseball field and is entirely fictional, this story proves that our own, individual dreams could spring to life, at any moment or in any setting.

It is my sincere hope that you, the reader, can benefit from the story, and for a brief moment, find yourself able to rekindle a small piece of the magical feeling that each of your childhood dreams instilled. Moreover, regardless of where this life takes you, please remember the words of William Arthur Ward: "If you can imagine it, you can create it. If you can dream it, you can become it."

CHAPTER 1

It was a cold, late October night with a strong north wind from Lake Michigan whistling its way inside the walls of historic Wrigley Field in Chicago. After three hours and twenty-six minutes, several unnerving moments, and a few botched calls, the contest had reached the bottom of the ninth. By that point in the evening, the game had already been a genuine spectacle to span generations.

The night had begun with Chicago's hometown favorite and lifelong Cub fan Richard Marx singing the National Anthem; in a special pregame tribute to the Armed Forces, Lee Greenwood had rendered a stirring performance of his classic, "God Bless the U.S.A."; and the stadium had honored three dozen former Cub and Red Sox ballplayers in attendance. Many celebrities found their way into the stadium, where they sat proudly rooting for their teams. The celebrities and Hall-of-Famers received no special treatment. Although many of the Hall-of-Famers filled the box seats behind home plate, the celebrities enjoyed and imbibed in the outfield bleachers, like the rest of the fans, including the trademark Chicago Cubs' "Bleacher Bums." There were no bad seats from which to watch the game, though many fans agreed that such a classic baseball pairing required seating in the historic center field bleachers. The game had been an epic duel between two of the sport's most notorious and esteemed competitors: a battle so action-packed that the replay film was destined to be an "Instant Classic," aired many times on the ESPN family of television networks and shown often in highlight clips on every major news channel and every local or regional sportscast in the days to come.

It was Game 7 of the World Series – the Chicago Cubs versus the Boston Red Sox. In the bottom of the ninth, two Cub runners auspiciously perched atop the bases at second and third and two batters had been retired. The crowd, rowdy all night, was suddenly as still as a feather beneath the starless, cloud-filled sky on Chicago's North Side.

The Cubs were trailing by two runs and the batter at the plate would become either a hero or a villain. Or should I say heroine or villainess?

Kimberly Reedeaux was the batter. Yes, you heard me correctly, Kimberly. A girl, a female, a vixen, a publicity stunt – you could have called her whatever you wanted; she had heard them all. A trim brunette, Kim's trademark style was a ponytail, always neatly and delicately pulled through the back of her ball cap. Many had deemed her more suited for ballet than baseball (at least that is what the sportswriters had said). However, once all of the criticism and rumors were set aside, one fact was clear: she had a mortar for an arm, capable of producing a lightning bolt of power.

Although tall and thin, Kim had solid muscle mass, rigid upper body strength, and firm hands that could hurl baseballs as well as they could lift baking pans from the oven. Devoid of the dainty features that most females are given, Kim's arms were more like artillery and she used them, on a daily basis, as such.

Raised by her parents and shaped, more specifically, by her father's influence, Kim came into this world as the only daughter of a small-market radio sportscaster from rural Minnesota. She held an appreciation for the game of baseball from the moment her eyes first saw daylight.

As a child, instead of *Green Eggs and Ham*, Kim drifted to sleep with the stories of Babe Ruth's controversial 1932 "Called Shot," Lou Gehrig's inspirational 1939 farewell speech, and Bobby Thompson's famous 1951 "Shot Heard 'Round the World." She excelled in mathematics by calculating batting averages. She learned to read with the aid of *Sports Illustrated* magazines.

By the end of her high school career, Kim could recite nearly every statistic of every ballplayer to have played the game from the 1930s through the 1980s, especially if they had played for the Cubs.

Yes, one might say that Kim loved baseball. She loved baseball so much that when she became too old for Little League, she changed the world. Kim could toss an 85-mph fastball and show up the rest of any male-dominated team. Such feats became Kim's way of proving that she could play and deserved to play ball with the guys.

In her senior year of high school, Kim received a full-ride scholarship to play softball for the University of Oklahoma. She turned down that offer to explore the possibilities that Chicago's Northwestern University would provide. Later, she forewent that goal to pursue a dream: becoming the first female to sign, play on, and start for a Major League Baseball club.

Kim did not want to set an example by becoming a ballplayer in some Major League team's Class A, AA, or AAA farm club; she wanted to land a starting job with the one of the Major League's professional ball clubs. She was not willing to settle for less than the top, even if that goal meant starting at the bottom, like every other individual to have played the game.

Many people had called her crazy for envisioning such an outlandishly absurd dream. After all, Major League Baseball had banned the signing of women to professional baseball contracts in 1952, twenty years before Kim was born.

Even now, there is a belief among some groups that females are a stubborn breed. If this was and still is the case, then Kimberly Reedeaux was the most obstinate female of them all. The best trained mule's stompin' and spittin' had nothing on Kim's will and even less on her heart. Many times in her life, she had known what she wanted and despite setbacks, she had always found a way to reach her goal.

When it came to her Major League Baseball dream, she always told a naysayer: "I'll change the laws; I'll make them better; I'll make them listen." Indeed, that was still her trademark answer when beset with questions by those who felt her Major League obsession was a joke. By the time that Kim's pursuit reached its finality, she was over forty years of age and she knew that time was stacked against her if she wanted to win it all. Time, however, was the only thing stacked against her.

From the moment she stepped from that high school stage with diploma in hand, Kim had fought a system. In baseball, the system focused exclusively on men. Women did not play baseball – plain and simple. At least, in Kim's day and age, they did not play professionally.

For over a century, women had benefited from certain roles in the sport. In 1866, Vassar College became the first university to create a women's baseball team. In 1898, twenty-year-old Lizzie Arrington became the first woman to sign a professional baseball contract. She played and pitched in one game for Class A Reading, Pennsylvania. From 1905 through 1911, Amanda Clement umpired for several semi-professional baseball teams. In 1931, seventeen-year old Jackie Mitchell signed with the Chattanooga Lookouts, a Minor League team in the Southern Association, and became remembered for striking out both Lou Gehrig and Babe Ruth in an exhibition game. From 1943 through 1954, the All-American Girls Professional Baseball League (AAGPBL) was in existence, and in 1974, Lanny Moss became the first woman baseball manager when she took charge of the Minor League Portland Mavericks team.

Despite this history, Major League Baseball had banned women. Kim, who as a high school graduate harbored such a lofty Major League dream, had known that she would have a battle on her hands to change the long-standing sense of normal in the sport. She was also aware that her fight for change would be a long and difficult one. But, in order to achieve her goal, she saw the task as a "minor inconvenience in a major league sense." The challenge she faced to rewrite the laws was not the first fight in her life. Over the years, before she would play in the biggest feat of her sports career – the World Series – she had faced innumerable obstacles and bested every hurdle.

Kim was the youngest child in a family of seven. Her parents, already struggling to make ends meet for their four sons, did not enjoy the thought of bringing another life into a situation already made difficult by the 1970s era economy. Kim's arrival certainly did not serve to ease the strain, especially because she was a health nightmare come true.

Kim was born nearly three months' premature in June 1972. The townspeople, of course, discussed her birth with criticism and gossip, saying that her parents were fools for having another child and that Kim would never be able to live a full life in the shadow of her early disabilities. They called her a freak and an outcast, but Kim never allowed their words to injure her spirit. She stood tall and firm, proving others' opinions wrong, time and again. When it seemed the entire world believed her crazy as she announced her dream to play professional baseball in the Majors, a few looked at her accomplishments to date and accepted that she was bound to excel.

In this late stage of her career, though, Kim found herself walking to home plate in a precarious position, with the outcome of the game depending on her insight, her skill, her sensibility, and her finesse. This could be the game of her life or the game that cost her life – the fans in Chicago had been awaiting this victory for over a hundred years. The team's cross-town rivalry with the White Sox meant that everything baseball occurring in the "Windy City" had fighting words attached to it, and the White Sox fans seemed to be the meanest of them all. The hapless Cubs, "loveable losers," Chicago's "North Side Farm Team," whatever you wished to call them, the ball club that called Wrigley Field "home" never seemed to receive much credit, all because of its history of letdowns.

The mentality of many residents became "Find me a Chicago resident who likes both the White Sox and Cubs and I'll show you someone that has not lived in Chi-town very long." The same philosophy applied to any other intra-city baseball rivalry. When two professional sports teams reside in one city, a town's fans and their loyalties divide. While a percentage of the community will pull for both teams, not very many are willing to go on record and admit dual loyalties.

The rivalries are one thing; this game was another. This was the Cubs' biggest and brightest chance to win the World Series for the first time in over 100 years. At long last, Kim's practice swings were done, her warm-up time through, and the moment – for which she had waited over four decades – was about to be hers.

The Friendly Confines of Wrigley Field soon filled with cheers and an occasional boo from visiting Red Sox fans. Kim's mind tried to drown the taunting just as she hoped to drown the 99-mph fastball of the great Leon Chapman. Yes, that Leon Chapman – the forty-six-year-old superstar who, three seasons earlier, had been dubbed as past his prime, and the one player in all of professional sports who felt there was no place for a woman beyond the "Friendly Confines" of the kitchen. The one and only Leon Chapman–strikeout king, Cy Young winner, shoe endorser extraordinaire, and sure-fire first-ballot Hall-of-Famer once his greed disappeared and he finally came to the conclusion that his playing days were better left to the dust of a mantel than the dirt of a pitching mound.

Thus, the scene was set: an All-Star pitcher with several rings on his fingers against "the girl," "the female," "the vixen," and "the ultimate baseball publicity stunt" in the battle of the current millennium with so much at stake. If Chapman could retire Kim, Red Sox fans, critics, and writers would hail him a hero, regaled not just for winning the ballgame – and the World Series – but for slaying the Cubs, a team "so long degraded that they resorted to calling up a female ballplayer in a lame attempt to win." At least, that's what the sportswriters would say.

CHAPTER 2

Kim stopped at home plate and glared into the eyes of the crafty Red Sox veteran. The crowd noise intensified as Leon began scraping at the dirt on the mound. Even the thick cloud cover of the night could not muffle the sounds. Win or lose, the Cubs faced critiques in the papers, on television, and across the radio airwaves the next day, but for now the fans' hopes and dreams were riding on the shoulders of their most unlikely player – Kim Reedeaux. The Cub fans began chanting her name, while the Red Sox faithful began shouting "Ree-deaux, Ree-deaux – soon the Cubs'll need a redo," a sad piece of wordplay on the shortstop's name.

The moon had hidden behind thick cloud cover three innings before the classic pitcher versus hitter duel emerged. Even now, years later, sports fans recall that a contest with such intensity was too much for even the moon's pulse to bear on that night. To that moment, the game had seen three ejections, including the Red Sox manager and pitching coach, two Gatorade coolers tipped end-for-end, and an earlier rain delay that did more to fuel the anger between the teams than to cool the heightened spirit. After all, it was the seventh game of the Fall Classic and nothing on this earth was more important to either team.

And there she was – Kim Reedeaux, all six-foot three-inches of her – standing with a bat in her right hand in the biggest game of her life, if not the lives of all Cub fans.

The history of the ball club was certain. On many an occasion, during the franchise's long World Series drought, the term "close but no cigar" had been uttered. By the early 1990s, those words in conjunction with "Wait till next year" had become as melodic as the sounds that streamed from the old Lowrey Heritage organ housed within the ballpark.

In the 1920s and 1930s, the Cubs had won four pennants but despite the power that Rogers Hornsby, Hack Wilson, and their teammates had brought to the table, the North Siders were never able to close the deal. In 1945, the Cubs lost to their fellow Midwesterners, the Detroit Tigers, in the seventh game of the World Series. In 1969, behind the talent of Ron Santo, Ernie Banks, Ferguson Jenkins, and Randy Hundley, the Cubs proved that even the wit and wisdom of their widely hailed and well-regarded manager, Leo Durocher, was not enough to secure a piece of baseball immortality. With a World Series berth a near certainty, the Cubs were eclipsed in September by the 1969 New York "Miracle" Mets, who went on to capture the both the pennant and the World Series.

In 2003, the Cubs found life behind a solid pitching staff, sound offensive play, and newly acquired manager Dusty Baker. The team won the National League Central Division and was, yet again, within an eyelash of baseball's main attraction before a botched outfield play and fan interference forced game seven, a game that the Cubs ultimately lost.

On this particular crisp and cool October night, however, all eyes focused on the present. The Billy Goat curse that tavern owner Billy Sianis reportedly placed on the Cubs the night in 1945 when he was asked to leave the World Series due to his pet goat's odor; the Black Cat curse in 1969 when a black cat strolled past the on-deck circle and Cubs great Ron Santo, distracting the game and reportedly leading to the later evaporation of the Cubs 1½-game division lead; and the "Bartman Ball," interference by Cub fan Steve Bartman with the Cubs just 5 outs away from the World Series in 2003; the opposing team's comebacks; and the Cubs' notorious meltdowns were not nearly as important as what was riding on the upcoming at-bat.

Over the course of a century, Cub fans had packed the Wrigley bleachers and seats within opposing teams' parks and rooted again for their beloved ball club. Generations of Chicago Cub fans heard stories of the good old days in the early 1900s when the Cubs were a regular baseball "dynasty," as we define the term today. Stories were shared about the rivalries, the chivalry, and the camaraderie, but nowhere written or shared in those tales was the one story that everyone so longed to hear – the story of the Cubs' destiny, the long, hard-fought battle against the worthy opponent in the most important of all games, the World Series. Few alive were old enough to remember such Cub greatness firsthand. Those who fantasized about the scene envisioned the Cubs perched proudly atop the championship ranks with their trusty bats, sturdy gloves, and solid defensive plays in tow. After all, the Cubs franchise had won the second-most games in all of professional baseball during the twentieth century, right behind the San Francisco Giants. And yet, a World Series victory was beyond the recollection of all but a few centenarians.

For the true Cub fan and his World Series dream, sound plays, smart at-bats, and superiority were the only ways to view being the best in the world. Now, in the early twenty-first century, very few Cub fans remembered first-hand the team's last World Series victory in 1908 or what drove the team's success. Regardless, thousands upon millions of die-hard, blue-collar faithful still flocked to Wrigley Field every spring and summer harboring the hope that "Next year is now." And with Kim Reedeaux at the plate, "now" was hopefully as soon as one long line drive away.

The critics that Kim Reedeaux encountered, through her solid season at shortstop, all seemed to have their eyes focused on her and yet she tried not to succumb to the pressure. Against all odds, she was a Major League Baseball player, just like her male counterparts on the field that night and all of the great male players who had come before her. Despite the crucial at-bat she was destined to take, Kim saw herself as nothing more than a teammate and baseball professional with an assigned task that she had every intention of completing. Her franchise had undergone over a century of both happiness and heartbreak without a World Championship, and her city was a forgiving sports town whose citizens had consistently thrown their support behind the Cubbies in good times and bad. Winning a hard-fought Game 7, in an equally difficult Fall Classic, was the most important duty of Kim's season.

After a few warm-up swings, she was ready for the task and dug in at home plate, at half past ten Central Time. Leon stood stoically on the pitcher's mound, trying his best to intimidate his opponent. He shifted his weight from right foot to left, straightened his cap at least fifteen times, and then hurled a wicked fastball toward home plate.

Most deemed it a clear-cut strike but the umpire, who possibly took pity on the girl, called it a ball. The Red Sox catcher chose to argue the call but to no avail. The count stood; one ball and no strikes.

Again, Leon twirled the baseball around in his glove as he reached into his mental bag of tricks to determine his next move. Leon Chapman had been around the league long enough to know what his manager and pitching coach thought would be best without their needing to tell him. He shook off his catcher and did so again before throwing another high fastball, a called strike. His next pitch was a third fastball that Kim got just a piece of, for a foul ball. As he set his position for his next trick, the lightning flashed, the thunder clapped, and the heavy rains poured with such force that clenching a baseball was next to impossible. The home plate umpire motioned to the grounds crew as the players hurried from the field. The only thing that Kim could do was sit and wait for a respite in the downpour.

Mother Nature had forced play to a proverbial standstill yet again, but the delay was the best thing that could have happened to Kim. The rain gave her a chance to relax, an opportunity to regroup, and a time to reflect upon the dirt and back roads, the high and low roads as well as the life and legal roads that led her to don one of the most coveted professional baseball jerseys and participate in the most sacred of all events – the World Series.

CHAPTER 3

It was 1976 – the year of the American Bicentennial. Nothing could have been more American than fireworks, hot dogs, and of course, Chicago Cubs baseball to celebrate the Fourth of July weekend. Harold Reedeaux, Kim's father, worked the morning shift at WWWI-AM in Brainerd, Minnesota. Having received the co-hosting job for the "Harold and Holt Morning Sports Show" shortly after graduating from Central Lakes College, Harold had been with the radio station for nearly sixteen years and had never taken a vacation, always tabling off-time for backyard playtime with his kids. Raising a family of seven on a small-market radio salary was not an easy task, especially in light of Kim's health issues. Thus, in work and in life, Harold always wanted more, but more – in the sense he wanted – never seemed to come.

Harold was certain, though, that 1976 would be the year to quench his need for more. To date, the year had treated his family well and granted him the opportunity of a lifetime. For all of his life, Harold had longed to see how the other half lived. A simple man, raised on equally simple principles, Harold worked his way through college by bagging groceries at his family's market and moonlighting for community radio part-time on weekends. He discovered a keen love for radio while pursuing his engineering degree, but the mentality of small-town politics and local sports was all he had ever known.

Like many citizens from small communities, Harold had big-time dreams. He wanted to live, work, eat, and drive in a big city. Generally speaking, Harold wanted to be big or find a life bigger than what he had known, not just for him but for his family. So, when the opportunity to utilize some vacation arose, Harold purchased two tickets: one airplane ticket from Minneapolis to LaGuardia airport and one ticket to the July 4, 1976, Chicago Cubs versus New York Mets game at Shea Stadium in Flushing, New York.

Harold was a Cub fan and had been for his entire life. His father, Louis, had been a White Sox devotee and Harold always guessed that is why he loved the Cubs – his Cub love gave Louis and Harold a father-son arguing point. In true childlike nature, Harold had embarked upon certain life choices just to spite his dad. The two were often at odds over the cross-town rivalry, even though they lived in rural Minnesota, two states and several hundred miles from the scene of their disagreement.

For Harold, life and work had always gotten in the way of actually attending a Cubs game. He had married his high school sweetheart, Elizabeth, while they were in college and they had immediately started their family, which meant that extra money was often unavailable. Harold and Elizabeth made up for what they could not financially provide through their love for their family, but baseball games and faraway trips always took a backseat to camping trips and television.

Until the summer of 1976, the closest Harold had gotten to Wrigley Field, his beloved Cubs, and the cherished ivy of green was the *Chicago Tribune* offices on the rare occasion that his work required travel. Traveling, work, and a growing young family never left time for play. He had never been to New York or done a spontaneous thing in his life until he planned his Bicentennial trip, a trip that would prove to be the first in a series of "spur of the moment" decisions.

The game was pegged as a classic (at least in the mind of a small-town sports anchor), pitting the old against the new. The Chicago franchise was nearly a century old, whereas the Mets had been a team for a little over a decade. Both teams had star players and the scene was set for a Sunday to remember.

Harold had settled into his seat about an hour before game time. Hot dog in hand and the smell of freshly cut grass tickling his nose, Harold perceived that his dream was coming true. Now, all he needed was a Cubs victory.

At the end of the 4th inning, with the Cubs trailing the Mets 5–1, Harold heard the words that would change him forever: "Excuse me." Harold turned around to see a tall, older, clean-shaven man wearing a Cubs' baseball cap and business attire. The man clenched a cane with one hand as he extended his other hand to Harold.

"Are you enjoying the game?" the stranger asked.

"I'm enjoying the scenery but the Cubs are behind," Harold replied, with a sense of inquisition.

"What do you think the Cubs are doing wrong?" the man prodded.

Harold, in trademark sportscaster jargon, proceeded to give the stranger a ten-minute dissertation about what the team could and should change.

"You're good," the man replied, after hearing Harold's analysis, "Ever work in media?"

Harold, visibly puzzled, nodded and was about to inquire why the man had taken such an interest in the game and him but was interrupted before he could ask.

"I am Wilbur Winchester, Mr…"

Harold introduced himself.

"I am the station manager of KDKA in Pittsburgh; I'm sure you've heard of us."

Of course Harold had heard of the radio station. Who hadn't? KDKA was the first commercial radio station in the country.

Wilbur did not allow Harold enough time to nod.

"Ever work for a large and popular sports and news talk radio station?"

"No, I've been at WWWI for all sixteen years of my radio career," Harold answered.

"You want to work for us; we'll pay you well."

Harold began to agree and then realized that six other people in his family needed to be consulted.

After Harold explained his family situation, Wilbur handed him a business card and told him to discuss the offer with his family and notify the station when a decision had been reached, either way.

Harold's discussion with Wilbur Winchester had spanned the last five innings of the baseball game. By the time Wilbur and Harold had finished speaking, the fans had begun to make their way from the stadium. Harold arose from his seat and exited the ballpark before noticing who was victorious.

"This is going to sound like a silly question," Harold asked a Mets fan, "but who won the game?"

The final score: Mets 9, Cubs 4. But to Harold, his trip to New York had suddenly become more about life and less about baseball.

Harold boarded the airplane for Minnesota just as fireworks were adorning the trademark New York skyline. In every shade of red and blue, he saw the future and that future appeared to reside in Western Pennsylvania. Little did he realize how a future in Western Pennsylvania would one day bring him closer to Wrigley Field and his Cubs than even he could have imagined.

CHAPTER 4

Harold arrived back home in Brainerd around 3:30 the next morning. With Minnesota locked in an unseasonably warm and dry period, the nighttime air felt like a sauna. The heat was so unbearable, even in darkness, that finding a full breath was next to impossible. When he entered the family home, Elizabeth was asleep on the couch. The children were resting on the floor, beneath the opened windows in the living room. While Harold had been away, the air conditioning had gone out again and the repairman quoted an overpriced bill that the family simply did not have the finances to pay. After all, Kim's surgeries had nearly drained their savings account and with five children, living paycheck to paycheck was not an easy task.

Harold went into the kitchen and poured a glass of milk. The light from the refrigerator was enough to awaken Elizabeth, who sleepily strolled to the dining room table. Harold sat and picked up the local newspaper, folding it into the shape of a fan.

"Are you okay?" Elizabeth asked him.

"I'm tired," Harold answered.

"Well, it was a long flight; how did the game go?"

"It was not so much the game, Lizzie," Harold began. "The Cubs lost but I was offered a job in Pittsburgh."

"Offered a job?" Elizabeth asked.

Harold explained the game, the meeting with Wilbur Winchester, and the job offer before waiting for what he had deemed as certain rejection from his wife.

"Let's get to packing!" Elizabeth said, with a glint of surprise.

"Really?" Harold asked. "What about the kids?"

"They're children, Harold," Elizabeth explained. "They may not understand now but we can provide a much better life for them if we can provide a happier and healthier life for ourselves. Nothing happens here. It never has; it never will. We should go where things happen."

By sunrise Harold and Elizabeth had already packed four boxes of the family's belongings. All of the children were awake by 9 a.m. and seated at the table for the announcement.

"We're moving to Pennsylvania," Elizabeth declared with a tear in her eye.

Two of the boys stormed out the door. The other two ran into their bedroom and slammed the door. Kim, a child of only four, grabbed a box and started placing her toys in it. She did not know where Pennsylvania was or what it meant to "pack up and move" but she knew if it had to be, she was going to have her stuffed teddies and bunnies ready, willing, and able to go.

Within three weeks, Harold, Elizabeth, and the children had packed their entire home, listed their two-story, three-bedroom brick home with a realtor, and were in a moving van headed for Pittsburgh. Mr. Winchester had pre-arranged their housing, given the unique circumstances that came with transporting a family of seven from Minnesota to Pennsylvania. The trip was long but with the help of baseball trivia by day and Eagles music by night, the time passed quickly. With each mile, Harold's outlook on the future seemed brighter and brighter.

Harold's mind began wondering as the midnight hour approached. He had stopped briefly to fill the moving van with gasoline and could see his children sleeping peacefully in the towed family sedan. As he stood in the heat, Harold closed his eyes and thought back to the 1940s and early 1950s when he was a young boy.

Back then, a young Negro family had moved into a predominantly white, rural Brainerd community. Harold never forgot their names – the Chaises: Norman, Nelda, and Nicky Chaise. Nicky was a teenager with a tremendous gift for baseball. Norman always said that the baseball gods reached down and gave Nicky a thunderbolt in the form of his left arm. Nicky was a pitcher who in today's society would have been drafted, straight from high school, gone on to play college ball (if he had not gone directly into the minors), and would have been a sure-fire candidate for no less than a number two starter's role on some Big League ball club's payroll. But Nicky's heyday was in the 1940s. Segregation was at its most prominent time, with entire towns split down the middle – African-Americans living on one side of the railroad tracks and Whites living on the other no intermingling accepted. For talented players like Nicky, a career in baseball meant either the Negro Leagues and off-season barnstorming or nothing at all. For a family-oriented child like Nicky, the decision was clear; the family came first and the dream was just a bunch of poppycock. Baseball was "only a game" to Nicky, even if it was a game that he loved.

So, when the need for a reasonable decision arose and he had to decide whether to pack his things and leave the farm to pursue the unrealistic goal of a Negro League career, something certain to be less than accepted by a good percentage of the nation, Nicky decided he stood a better chance of acceptance by becoming a hard-working farmer.

Nicky remained on the family's land until his father passed during the Korean Conflict in 1953. His mother died a short time later and by then, Jackie Robinson had broken the color barrier in baseball, leading to more than one hundred fifty African-American Major League Baseball players and the inevitable end of Negro League Baseball. Nicky, at age twenty-six, tried out for the Brooklyn Dodgers team but years of working on the farm had taken their toll on his back, his knees, and his legs. Thus, his dream remained just that – an idea that never made it to reality.

Jackie Robinson signed with the Brooklyn Dodgers in 1947, just five years before Major League Baseball's written ban of women in professional, competitive play. As Harold stood outside of his family's sedan, he peered in the window where his young daughter slept. He wondered why in a world where doors continuously open for change, baseball closed the door to the thought of women playing the game.

Just as the mentality that had surrounded African Americans vanished, so too had the idea that a woman's place remained solely in the home. Women worked in factories and refineries, restaurants and hotels, and traveled the world as proud, committed members of the United States military's four branches. Certainly, there were still many women who preferred to be stay-at-home housewives and mothers, large tasks in their own right. A few short years later when she boarded the Space Shuttle, Sally Ride proved by jetting off to explore the unknown that some women could not be tied to home by any medium in this universe.

To Harold, the idea that it was acceptable for women to be battalion members but not battery mates in professional baseball seemed somewhat odd. Yet, what he did not know on the mid-August night in 1976 was that years later, his youngest child, and only daughter, would become the motivating voice behind the change he so longed to see.

CHAPTER 5

Being the only daughter of a sportscaster sometimes proved to be a difficult arrangement, however big or small the sports market was. In rural Minnesota, most of the sports radio discussions centered on high school sports rankings and more specifically, football season. It didn't matter if it was the fifth of April; the outlook for the upcoming football season was on the caller's mind. Different areas of the country had their other sports interests, such as basketball, track, or golf, but by day's end in nearly every small town of these United States, the talk would eventually turn to football.

In Minnesota, baseball was a second-class citizen to hockey. Most of the time, the weather was more suited for indoor activities than warm-weather sports. Even the Minnesota Twins played their games in a domed stadium. The state's bitter chill often thrived well into the summer months creating an early fall season that sometimes hit by mid-August.

If a young girl carried an appreciation for hockey, she was a goddess and certainly dating material. If she loved baseball, she was an outcast. For Kim Reedeaux, the criticism during her brief four-year residence in the Gopher State was enough to take its toll. It was one thing to have arrived into the world under delicate circumstances, completely out of her control. It was an entirely different dilemma to have conquered those obstacles, only to create more for herself by showing an early tendency toward loving nine innings of grown men girding their loins for a six-month season of throwing a ball, catching a ball, and hitting a ball.

The basic rules of baseball are so simple. Yet, when a questionable call occurs, the attempts made to determine who is right, the manager or the umpire, often made an easy game seem difficult.

Harold always believed the rules alone were why baseball was never "a woman's game." Just as there is an inherent fear of mathematics ingrained within many women's heads at a young age, it seemed to Harold as though the heavy emphasis on batting averages, pitch counts, and records, tied in with mathematics, left women scrambling for calculators when in reality, a deep love for the game was the most important aspect.

Something about baseball is simply inspiring. I don't think anyone is certain what the single-most inspirational aspect is. Everyone has differing opinions of the game itself and most have varied reasons for their personal "love" for the game of baseball. Not even the world's most seasoned poet could ever pinpoint a lone answer for why there is such an appreciation for nine men who place themselves on a grassy field and stand as one, for the sake of personal pride. Was the reason something greater? Did the love of baseball bring us closer to immortality? Therein was the question sure to reign throughout eternity, a question argued often and yet there was no explanation for it. The fan and the ballplayer, of course, had their own differing reasons for their "love of the game."

For some fans, the records draw them to the game. After all, some long-standing baseball records may remain for all eternity by the uniqueness and gravity of their feats. For other fans, the reasons for loving the game are simpler. Their haven is the smell of the freshly cut grass, the lights, the sounds, or the intensity that comes when a nine-inning duel between two hitting or pitching powerhouses lives to see an extra inning or two (or ten) before one team or the other comes out victorious.

As early as three years old, Kimberly's love – catching – was quite clear. On many a foggy morning in Minnesota, Harold would call for his boys and together, the four older siblings and he would head to the yard for a little game of catch. Like clockwork, at least once in the game, there was Kim, dressed in a pink, ruffled dress and adorned in pigtails, running in front of her brother to catch a long, overthrown baseball. Her family was surprised to learn that she was a natural-born righty. And, not to anyone's surprise, when the Reedeaux family arrived in their new home on the outskirts of Pittsburgh, Kim was the first to ask about a public park or some other place where she could challenge her brothers (or any boys, for that matter) to a game of catch.

Kim would dare anyone and that may have been due to all of the life-based "curveballs" she had to face as a preemie. But, girls, boys, their parents, their friends, even their dogs, were "challenge victims" if they chose to come between Kim and baseball.

While most elementary school–aged girls dreamed of becoming the next supermodel or "Super Mom," Kim's first childhood dream was to follow in her father's footsteps and go into broadcasting. However, in never wanting to settle for second best, Kim wanted to take her father's achievement one step further and join the ranks of the great television analysts whom she had admired throughout her young life.

By the time Kim was seven her favorite TV sports anchor was Al Michaels. Although her family had moved to Pittsburgh from Minnesota four years earlier, their true appreciation for hockey was still apparent. So, obviously, when the February 22, 1980, "Miracle on Ice" hockey game was won by the Americans, Kim's family was watching the game on television; they were just as ecstatic as every other American family and yet as stunned as the Russians and the world. Considering her father's sports anchoring background, Kim had a predisposition for great broadcasting. In baseball, she admired Vin Scully's ability to weave stories from the game of baseball into real-life accounts of those behind-the-scenes persons who made the game great. Her all-time favorite call, however, was one of the greatest sports "calls" of all time: Kim had always admired Al Michaels for his "Do you believe in miracles…Yes!" account at the end of that historic 1980 Olympic semi-final hockey game.

Did Kim "believe in miracles?" Yes, and as she sat on a hard, pine bench at Wrigley Field in late October, and watched the rain pour heavily from the black, desolate sky, she realized the miracle she had been given – the gift of baseball – while she dreamed that her brother, Brian, could have been there to see it.

The eldest of Harold and Elizabeth's five children, Brian was a tall, lanky boy with reddish-brown hair and freckles. As a child he had a sheer appreciation for all things out-of-doors. In the winter, he would partake in everything from backyard ice hockey to skiing. In the spring, he was a star runner and budding track champion. In the summer, he would awaken at dawn and gather his fishing pole and minnows with one goal in mind – to find the most unsuspecting fish in the big river and bring him home as his trophy for the day. In the fall, Brian had aspirations of becoming the next "Joe Greene."

Harold had always questioned his son's football playing goals, certain that Brian was better skilled for a career in hockey than spending, or wasting, his time as a defensive tackle. Through the eyes of a father, Harold's opinions seemed well-meaning but to a very opinionated thirteen-year-old such as Brian, the very thought that he "could never be Joe Greene" was not a suggestion that sat easily on the heart.

Of course, that led to an occasional rift between father and son. Over time, the rifts became more and more and the rebellion became worse and worse, until Brian turned sixteen, received his driver's license, tattooed his family members' names on his arm as a memory, and sped off into the sunset, vowing never to return again.

Brian's loss affected each member of the Reedeaux family. The three remaining Reedeaux boys, Kelly, Kristopher, and Kevin, missed their brother and subconsciously blamed their father as the reason that Brian left. For Harold and Elizabeth, the void meant an unpleasant memory, every night, as dinner time came with an empty seat at the table.

For Kim, Brian's departure was the epitome of all things bad. He was not only her big brother but also her best friend. Brian had been the host for her tea parties, her defender when her other siblings, through rough-housing, chose to attack, and her closest confidant. Brian and Kim were close and his choice to leave the family and head out on his own was devastating to her.

In the thirty years that had passed since Brian left, the family had always hoped and prayed that he would write a letter, place a phone call, or give them some indication that he was alive and well, both healthy and happy. The day had never come but each year at Christmas, five minutes of silence were set aside in honor of the time Brian would have spent opening presents. It was a somber time and yet something that served to bring each family member closer together and closer to Brian.

Kim wiped a mascara-stained tear from her eye as she looked upon the medium-sized rain droplets beating down, in rhythmic time, upon the large blue tarp that covered the grounds of Wrigley Field. She loved the game of baseball and had fought a gallant fight to be in uniform that day. Still, if she could have traded it all for one thing, just one thing in the world, she would have chosen her brother. She missed her sparring partner, her fishing buddy, but most of all, she missed her friend.

CHAPTER 6

Baseball records are like a child's cherished teddy bear collection; if you're the record-holder, you admire and coddle them. While it is human nature for everyone else to want the record that is so rightfully yours, you dread the very thought of someone coming along to take your precious record away.

It does not matter if the record is for the number of hits in Little League or consecutive at-bats in the Majors; a baseball record is a baseball record. Praised by fans, worldwide, in the universal language of the game, baseball records are sacred.

In 1983, Kim Reedeaux, as an eleven-year-old, performed a feat that to this day, no other girl in America has ever attempted, let alone succeeded at; she hit a grand slam home run in a Little League game. At that time, nine years had passed since the Little League rules were changed, leading to girls being allowed to compete.

Kim's record-setting grand slam event was a first for Little League Baseball and set a benchmark for future generations of girls to follow. The sport's rule change would, yet again, prove as beneficial the next year when Victoria Roche, of the 1984 Belgium Little League team, became the first girl to play in the annual World Series, held in Williamsport, Pennsylvania.

By the mid-1980s, the popularity of Little League baseball had grown to unprecedented heights and the inclusion of girls on participating teams served to increase not only the popularity but also the exposure of baseball.

Media giant ABC Television aired live the final 1985 Little League World Series game, and from that time onward, the audience increased for witnessing children play the sport of baseball for the fun, thrill, and admiration for the game.

By 2003, Little League Baseball had grown to see 2.3 million children, aged nine to twelve, in 104 countries and all fifty of these United States, compete in Little League play. Yet, in the approximately twenty years that had passed since Kim Reedeaux's grand slam, no one had ever come close to eclipsing her record.

Kim's "Grand Slam Day" in 1983 was a crisp, clear, and cool day for late summer. The weather in the Pittsburgh area appeared to be setting up for an early autumn. Though it was August 12th, the trees had already begun showing signs of becoming the glorious shades of reds, yellows and oranges that so many people longed to see, year after year.

The bright eleven-year-old awakened early that morning and had already run thirty laps around her backyard by the time the rest of her family followed suit. On that day, Kim's team – the Bluebonnet All-Girls Little Leaguers – would play Upton, an all-boys team that had won the 1982 State Championship. Kim knew that those boys were large and skilled and that her team of "pixies," as they had called themselves, would need some "fairy dust" in order to conquer the challenge. Their coach, Jeffrey Johnson, had scheduled the game for two reasons. One, he wanted to prove that his girls were every bit as qualified as Upton's boys when it came to the fundamentals of the game, and two, let's face it: we do live in a society where being beaten by a girl is not an honor that many boys, regardless of age, like to admit.

The game had been on the All-Girls team schedule for nearly a season. For just as long, Coach Johnson had been schooling his girls on the game of baseball as if he had been preparing them for a "pass the test or fail the grade" standardized school examination. He taught them to bunt better, field surer, run faster, and dive harder. The girls knew so many different signs for the various baseball plays that if American Sign Language were all about baseball, the Bluebonnets would have the art mastered to a tee.

You may think it was rather silly for a coach to push his girls so hard. After all, the game was and still is just that, a game, at the Little League level of play. Coach Johnson's decision, however, was not about taking the fun from the game; it was about making a point.

Since the 1982 Little League Championship, the Upton Boys Little League team had been media darlings. Television stations from as far south as Morgantown, West Virginia, as far east as New York City, as far west as Cincinnati, Ohio, and as far north as Montreal, Quebec, in Canada had traveled to the Pittsburgh area to cover the story. Just as many newspaper reporters and radio sports shows were involved in covering the tale. Even Harold Reedeaux, who, thanks to his daughter, would so soon go from sports anchor to media enemy, was in charge of covering the Upton story for KDKA-AM.

The Upton team's 1982 season had been a harrowing account of sheer heart. Two years before, a nine-year-old boy named Rich Robards had arrived at the Upton summer practice camp. Rich came to the practice session with flip-flop style shoes and braces on his legs. He walked with crutches and until the boys on Upton's team got to know and understand Rich, they thought he was a poor kid, just wasting his time.

Rich Robards was a twin. His brother died shortly after birth and his own birth complications left him with a disability. He was born and lived with a left clubfoot. His father, Ralph, was a plant worker but cutbacks and layoffs in the steel industry during the late 1970s forced him to the unemployment lines. The family's finances waned. While Ralph Robards would have sacrificed everything in his life for his family, sensibility still remained the most important faction. With the quoted surgery to repair his son's clubfoot ranging from ten to fifty thousand dollars, and insurance that had lapsed due to sky-high premiums, there was simply not enough money to cover such an extreme.

Rich's parents, in light of his brother's death, tried desperately to give him as normal a life as he could possibly enjoy, in spite of his obvious disability. So it was that in 1980 when Rich had read about the Upton baseball camp, his parents paid the money for the session, drove him to the ball field, and watched as he maneuvered his way, crutches and all, through the crowds of eager children.

Even the faintest of heart on the baseball field that day had to stop for a moment to admire Rich's courage. He was there, not only as a participant in the camp, but as an inspiration to all children with disabilities.

Rich made the Upton Little League team, not as a player, but as the designated "water boy." He was the reason behind the media frenzy. The excitement surrounding the 1982 State Championship that Upton had garnered was real but more of the media personnel were interested in Rich's story than a simple game of balls and strikes.

Despite their 1982 State Little League Championship, the Upton team proved themselves to be bad sports. The ball players, from the moment they learned of the meeting with the girls' team, had become miniature tyrants. Some of the players had sprayed shaving cream on the windows of the opposing girls' homes; others had made a mockery of the players' front yards by way of toilet paper, paper towels, and other household items.

Rich's story, over the past two years with the Upton team, was a nice one and a story that, certainly, more teams should consider when choosing how best to accommodate disabled athletes, but he was just the water boy and was not a factor in the upcoming battle.

Nearly the same boys' roster from the prior year was playing in the game, written in the Pittsburgh area newspapers as the Little League version of the Billie Jean King versus Bobby Riggs tennis match-up of the previous decade. Of course, Kim, her teammates, her family, and her friends genuinely hoped that the outcome of the Little League game would prove to have the same result as that historic tennis game. Yet, whatever the level, as everyone involved in a sporting event knows, the object of the game should be less about winning and losing and more about how one plays the game.

The temperature was a pleasant fifty-nine degrees when Kim arrived at the stadium that mid-August afternoon. The baseball field had been recently cut and the bleachers were packed with several hundred adoring fans, eager for the "David and Goliath" meeting.

While Kim had enjoyed the art of being a baseball catcher during the backyard brawls with her brothers, she had the duty of playing the shortstop position for her Bluebonnet team. As in every other facet of her life, Kim played the position with all the heart and pride she could muster, never leaving anything to question when she walked from the field at game's end. If one were to look up the term "Little Leaguer's heart" in an encyclopedia, Kim's picture would accompany the listing. The girl had class, spirit, and of course, tremendous talent that went above and beyond the normal skill level of the average Little Leaguer.

Some people believed that Kim's humble yet competitive nature was the result of her father's career in radio, and that may have well been the case. Radio personalities must achieve some sense of poise and charisma in order to attract and keep their listeners. The individual radio personality's career and his ability to retain employment are contingent upon ratings, and ratings hinge on how he comes across to his audience. If a listener does not trust the sports broadcaster chatting with him, he quits listening.

Kim's "audience" was the fan base that she shared with her teammates, and while she was only eleven years old, she appreciated the fact that if her team played poorly, the fans' support of the "Bluebonnet" League would dwindle.

Her father, through sharing his radio-related stories, had taught Kim the life's wisdom he had learned while spending his days and nights calling balls and strikes behind a microphone, and one could have said that Harold Reedeaux's young pupil had learned well. Still, those beliefs were just the opinions that others had formed when they looked upon a young girl whom many had deemed odd. After all, she showed relentless appreciation for a "man's game."

However, to those relatives, friends, and townspeople who actually knew Kim, the motivation behind her every move was quite clear. She longed to give back a small portion of her life's blessings to her team and her coaches, each and every game. By the end of that day, she would give her team, her coaches, and her community a story to far eclipse that of the Upton Little League Champions.

With the wee people "Battle of the Sexes" scheduled for 2:30, the Little League umpiring crew would not stand for tardiness. Of course, the girls arrived with plenty of time to spare. As the "underdogs," the "Pixies" wanted to have a final workout before the game.

The fact that the team wanted a final warm-up was not nearly as surprising as the scene that unfolded on the field during that workout. The girls synchronized their warm-ups. Each girl turned, threw, and fielded at the same moment. The team looked as though they had been playing the game much longer than their ages suggested.

The boys sauntered into the stadium at 1:45 for a 2:30 game and barely had enough time to stretch before the first pitch. The Pixies won home-field advantage, even though the turf was neutral to both ball clubs. I guess the umpires felt the need to take pity upon the girls as well.

The first four and a third innings were rather uneventful. There was one sacrifice fly ball that nearly became a home run for the Upton team but other than that, the game was a duel and neither side was willing to fold. With just one and two-thirds innings remaining in the contest, the stage was being set for what appeared to be an extra-inning affair.

In the top of the 6th inning, on a 2–2 count, a wiry, lanky boy named David Duhomme of the Upton team launched a curveball from the Bluebonnets' exhausted pitcher over the fence for a solo home run. The next batter, Donny Dixon, fired a high fastball to right field, scoring the team's second run. All hope for the Bluebonnet girls' team appeared to be lost.

In the bottom of the 6th, the girls had their best athletes up to bat. Krystal Copeland had been an All-Star in the Girls League, three years running; Devon McKeel was an all-around good athlete who played baseball in the summer and basketball in the winter; and Tara Daniels, while new to the team, had been playing baseball since she was strong enough to grip the ball. The best scenario for the "Pixies" was for one girl to get on base. With one runner on-base, Kim too would have an at-bat.

Krystal came to the plate, armed with a genuine Easton metal bat and one goal in mind – find first base. She was able to take the count to 3–2 before arching a fly ball over the first baseman's head and commanding a single.

Next, in a move that the Upton fans today still do not understand, their All-Star pitcher chose to intentionally walk Devon, who had played a solid game all day. Maybe the call occurred because she had played so well but there was good reason to question the free pass.

Tara Daniels became the third batter to hit in the inning. The still-discussed rumor is that Devon walked because the Upton coach did not believe Tara could hit. The problem was that everyone knew Kim was a power hitter and therefore Tara's ability was somewhat of a moot point. The danger within the Pixies' order was still looming and if Tara were to reach first, the bases would be loaded. Sure enough, on a wild pitch that went over the Upton catcher's head, Tara made her way to first base. The game rode on the next at-bat. Kim had the potential to do something that no other girl had ever done in Little League play – belt a Grand Slam homer.

Upton called their right fielder, Matt Burgess, to the pitcher's mound for his equally amazing fastball and slider capabilities. The first pitch was low and outside, though called a strike. The second pitch that Kim faced was waist high and right down the middle, yet she swung and missed. With an 0–2 count on the Pixies' star shortstop, the Upton bench began to cheer and their pitcher broke out his most devious grin. The other dugout, filled with her Pixies' teammates, began chanting obsessively for their crafty teammate and Kim knew exactly what she had to do.

Burgess stood on the mound and softly nodded; he had his sign and the rest was out of his control. He twirled the baseball around in his glove and then firmly planted his foot for the delivery.

For the onlookers in the Upton cheering section, the seconds between when the ball left Matt's glove and the time that it reached the plate seemed like hours and the moments only became longer from there. With a hefty heave, Kim swung and connected with the ball. The Upton outfielders ran quickly toward the wall but it was no use. Destiny had called that day and it called for Kimberly Reedeaux. With that grand slam, she became the first girl in Little League play to crush a round-tripper, but more importantly for her team of ten-, eleven-, and twelve-year-olds, they had slain a mighty giant.

That day in 1983 had been historic and the accomplishment afforded to Kim, then an eleven-year-old athlete, was of paramount importance. Yet, as Kim sat all alone on a bench in the Cubs' dugout, dressed in a Major League uniform, and harboring the knowledge that one at-bat, her at-bat, could, yet again, have historic value, she wanted one thing and one thing alone – a break in the clouds.

CHAPTER 7

In the early 1940s, the United States was knee deep in World War II. Baseball, the American Pastime, appeared headed toward a brief, yet certain, trek to the back burner of national importance.

Whereas in today's society, men as young as eighteen are drafted straight from high school and signed to Minor League baseball contracts, during the height of World War II, young men turning eighteen were being drafted to the four main branches of the military.

For these men, surviving with life and limb intact during a bleak and bitter war season was their focus and their championship. Each soldier knew his well-being would not come until the battle was complete and freedom was once again obtained. Balls and strikes gave way to guns and knives, and enraged umpires gave way to enemy strongholds.

By the fall of 1942, baseball franchises across the country had begun to feel the crunch that came from having the "Boys of Summer" serving overseas. Fearing an imminent collapse of the sport that had been a stepping stone of hope in the post-Depression era, Phillip K. Wrigley, Jr., who had recently inherited the Chicago Cubs club from his father, scoured the landscape for any feasible way to keep the game alive.

With the financial assistance of Mr. Wrigley, a small group of Midwestern businessmen founded the All-American Girls' Professional Baseball League (AAGPBL). The League consisted of teams in four Midwestern cities, governed by new, female gender–specific rules for the game. Each team had fifteen players, a manager, a business manager, and a chaperone; national sports figures became managers for the League with the hope that their following would help to spark interest in the league.

Spring Training for this new league began in mid-May 1943 and the regular season began a brief two weeks later. By the end of the 1943 season, more than 176,000 fans had attended AAGPBL games.

In 1944, the League expanded to six teams and the previous year's popularity in the sport proved that allowing the women to play in Major League stadiums was becoming a worthy and profitable venture.

The AAGPBL expanded again in 1946 and though the war had been over for a year, the attendance records for the League's eight teams continued to improve and impress AAGPBL ownership. On July 4, 1946, the All-American Girls' Professional Baseball League enjoyed a new record when ten thousand fans arrived to witness a double-header in South Bend, Indiana.

By 1949, four years after World War II had ended, life in America had returned to the pre-war sense of normalcy. Fans had begun to follow the careers of Joe DiMaggio, Ralph Kiner, Stan Musial, and Jackie Robinson via televised coverage and had all but forgotten such names as Bonnie Baker, Shirley Jameson, Clara Schillace, and Ann Harnett – four of the nearly 600 women who participated in the All-American Girls' Professional Baseball League that fans had flocked to see during the war years.

In 1952, Major League Baseball introduced a second ban on women participating in the sport. The original ban, written in 1931 by baseball's first commissioner, Kennesaw Mountain Landis, occurred days after seventeen-year-old Jackie Mitchell struck out Lou Gehrig and Babe Ruth in an exhibition game. The 1931 ban ruled that baseball was "too strenuous" for a woman to play. The Major Leagues terminated the contract tendered to Mitchell soon thereafter.

In light of the secondary ban and declining revenue for women's baseball, the All-American Girls Professional Baseball League disbanded in 1954, after celebrating eleven years of success.

Supporters of the ban had fought long and hard to keep the ruling solid. Over the course of the next forty years, several women's groups petitioned courts, nationwide, to hear the case with the hope of overturning baseball's ruling. But, until Kimberly Reedeaux came onto the scene in the mid-1980s, no one had been successful.

Kim's baseball-ridden battle with the court systems began on a local level in 1988 when she was barely old enough to drive. She was a Brentwood High School sophomore with a pristine grade point average and more talent than half of the boys in Allegheny County, Pennsylvania. Funding concerns forced her school to end the softball program. That move was, of course, a great one for cutting educational spending but while aiding the budget, the move left young women in the area settling for track and nothing else, if they chose to participate in a spring sport. Baseball was a boys' sport and the Brentwood School District's policy was quite clear in hammering home that point. The policy stated that no girls, not a single one, could participate in high school baseball games.

The policy also impacted practice. Female students were taboo on the practice field and the baseball field. During the season, they were not even allowed to be anywhere near the track surrounding the field during baseball practice – no exceptions. It did not matter if a spring track meet was approaching and a girl needed to prepare with the assistance of the hurdles; no exceptions meant absolutely zero exceptions.

The decision angered the parents of many female students. A group of these disgruntled parents joined together and attended multiple school board meetings regarding the topic of their daughters and baseball; still, by the end of each assembly, the rule firmly stood. The school board meetings seemed to be the end of the road for the idea of giving Brentwood girls equal representation in athletics. The higher powers present within the community had made their point that baseball held no place for a woman, in spite of the great popularity of the sport among the fairer sex. Many community activists, however, were not willing to accept that policy as the administration's "final answer."

To ensure equal representation and/or opportunity for women in sports, Title IX laws had gone into effect in 1972. Much attention was given to assure equal representation for female athletes in colleges across the country, yet there was still a great lack of compliance with the law when it came to high schools.

The argument by parents and female athletes in the Brentwood community centered on the premise that Little League baseball, per the sport's 1974 rule change, allowed female athletes to participate in once male-dominated sporting events. Therefore, the parents felt the school officials' adamant stance about banning women athletes from high school was in direct violation of the law. The school administration's take on the matter seemed to hold a double standard and ultimately served to leave girls hung out to dry, so to speak. The administration had basically told the parents in Brentwood that their daughters could be baseball players from age nine through twelve in the Little League program and could play alongside the boys on the junior high baseball team but after that, they were better suited to either knit or to take up basketball.

The days when a woman's job was solely in the home were a good forty years removed from society and yet, in Brentwood, those darker times for women were as present as the popularity of Madonna's music.

Many things inspired Kim Reedeaux: the changing of the seasons, the sunshine, the smell of freshly cut grass, the inquisitive nature of toddlers, and the popping sound of an aluminum baseball bat, or the cracking sound of a wooden one, as it connected with a ball. Most importantly, Kim found inspiration in the need for change and her compassion toward the needs of others.

If Kim uncovered a hurdle, she jumped it. If she came to a brick wall, she scaled it. If Kim saw a problem that required someone else's attention – a task too great for her alone to fix – she gathered support and challenged it. In this particular case, the sheer lack of Title IX compliance was motivation enough for her to become involved.

Some residents called her a radical, others called her a dreamer, but no one called her ruthless. Kim was a person who had come up against her own personal, yet private obstacles for nearly two decades and she was never one to accept the term "no" lightly.

Baseball surrounded her life from day one; sixteen years later, she was not in the frame of mind to give up the sport or the basic skills that she had long tried to perfect. Kim decided if changing the school district's baseball policy were to happen, which she strongly believed it should, she would have to be the one who led the charge. On a late fall day, with the help of her father's media ties, she began her mission.

Kim's first quest was research. With the assistance of her girlfriends in her high school journalism class, Kim lobbied for and received an off-season, after-school internship at the *Pittsburgh Tribune-Review* newspaper. Through her internship, she began an investigation into the Title IX–related practices in not just Brentwood but all of the Pittsburgh area high schools. Her mission began with seeing how well the rule was enforced.

Through her investigation, Kim examined the policies of the 129 public high schools in the Western Pennsylvania Interscholastic League and the Pittsburgh City League. Besides equal participation, Kim examined travel expenses for sports programs, uniform budgets for both genders, and whether or not the coaches' salaries for boys and girls sports were comparable. Her goal was to show Brentwood School District officials that a great discrepancy was apparent and therefore, the Brentwood community was in direct violation of the Title IX ruling.

Kim's findings were astonishing. In every school district and in every sport throughout the region housed in the Western Pennsylvania Interscholastic League, there was a difference of as much as $50,000 between boys' and girls' athletics.

In Kim's Brentwood community, the numbers showed a true imbalance. While 47.28% of the student-athletes in Brentwood were girls, only 30.34% of the total athletic budget went to women's athletics, with no money budgeted for girls' baseball.

"And this shows balance?" Kim asked herself as she sifted through pages upon pages of damning data. Still, even as stunning as the statistics were, many Brentwood girls did not want to fight the system. While these girls did not agree with the way things were, they were willing to accept the rulings as "what had always been done."

"What had always been done" – a statement that Kim Reedeaux hated. It was a statement that her great-grandmother had used. Every time Kim would ask her "Nana" why something was done a certain way, her great-grandmother would inevitably say, "I don't know; that's the way it has always been done."

Kim was a believer in transformation. When a situation arose in which something that had seemed to work for years was no longer adequate, Kim Reedeaux vowed to change it, whether the reason surrounded sports or not.

In 1984, Kim volunteered her time assisting an elderly lady whose home was in desperate need of cleaning. The woman, ravaged by arthritis and nearly unable to walk, lived alone, had no family, and their community dubbed her as everything from a bitter recluse to a charity case. As someone always judged but never judgmental, Kim befriended the woman and over the course of the next three weeks singlehandedly cleaned the neglected apartment from ceiling to floor and wall to wall. In turn, Kim gained a friendship that lasted until the woman's death in 1992; she had given the woman a small bit of hope in light of the woman's sad health condition.

Kim Reedeaux loved baseball and she knew that other girls from her Little League Bluebonnet team had grown fonder of the game as time had progressed. Armed with her newfound knowledge and with what she had classified as "hard evidence" for her claim of gender bias toward boys' sports, Kim attended the next school board meeting and discussed her findings with the panel.

The meeting was so ill-received by the Brentwood school officials that three board members nodded off to sleep during Kim's presentation and two others constantly interrupted her while she was sharing the irrefutable statistics. The board agreed to take the matter of equality under advisement, but Kim knew what that actually meant: the panel had no intention of addressing the matter again.

Kim had put off utilizing her father's media position out of respect for his job and through wanting to demonstrate her early sense of independence. But, when all else had failed, Kim did the only thing she could do – she went to the station and voiced her concerns via her father's radio program. In doing so, Kim shared her feelings with KDKA's morning listeners.

She chose the popular six o'clock hour – the heart of the early morning drive time – for her discussion and her father gladly accommodated. Kim knew that by going public with the claim, she was not only setting herself up for problems with the school district but also possibly jeopardizing her father's career, since any media outcry would be looked upon as his problem. Her father did not mind and agreed that blatant gender discrimination was occurring. Harold did not like discrimination in any form. During the time when many believed Whites and Blacks should not mingle, he had befriended the Chaise family.

As predicted, the radio station and school administration office's phone lines lit up after Kim's on-air segment. The residents of the communities surrounding the Pittsburgh area seemed completely unaware of the problem in their respective area school districts until Kim gave them the solid facts.

Over the course of the next few weeks, the school board in Brentwood, under heavy community and media scrutiny, invited Kim back for another meeting and three months to the day after that meeting, Kim and the female athletes at Brentwood High School got more than what they had bargained for. The school district still did not allow female athletes to participate in boys' baseball but instead, in partnership with the Western Pennsylvania Interscholastic League, they formed an all-new girls' baseball division, consisting of nearly one hundred teams in the Pittsburgh area.

From that point forward, Kim was dubbed as "the little shortstop that could" by her classmates and the community. Her conviction to fight the system, which had for so long been stacked against her, had hurled her into the local and national spotlight. In the months to come, the magnitude of her choice and the effect that it had on others began to become clear. By late fall that year; Kim had received hundreds, if not thousands, of letters from high school athletes nationwide. Some of the letters praised her decision to stand strong behind her beliefs; others criticized her for being so vocal, but Kim had seen her life and motives questioned since day one and her most recent action would only serve to be the beginning. The hardest test and strongest criticism were yet to come.

CHAPTER 8

From the day that she was old enough to comprehend the purpose of a television set and the point of nine men taking to the field with a common goal of winning, Kim was in love with Chicago Cubs baseball. The love was something passed down to her by her grandmother and father. While many children went out of their way to do the exact opposite of what their parents enjoyed, Kim embraced her father's admiration for both the baseball franchise and their stadium: beautiful, storied, and celebrated Wrigley Field.

Wrigley Field, Major League Baseball's second oldest ballpark and one of its smallest, rests between West Addison Street, North Sheffield Avenue, West Waveland Avenue, and North Clark Street in Chicago. The stadium opened on April 23, 1914, and a little less than two years later, the Chicago Cubs held their first contest at baseball's "Friendly Confines."

While undersized in comparison to other Major League stadiums, Wrigley Field has a rich history and a wonderfully portrayed tradition. The innovations tested and tried in the stadium near Lake Michigan paved the way for many of the advancements seen in larger baseball venues today.

The Chicago Cubs' home field was the site of the first pregame singing of "The Star Spangled Banner." The performance came prior to game one of the 1918 World Series, a Series which the Cubs lost to the Red Sox, four games to two. The first permanent concession stand in baseball arrived at Wrigley Field in 1914. In 1941, the Cubs' organization was the first in baseball to entertain their fans with organ music, a tradition that continues more than seventy years later. The custom of allowing fans to keep foul balls began at Wrigley Field, as did the custom of throwing back the opposing team's home run balls. Millions of fans worldwide have enjoyed singing "Take Me Out to the Ballgame" during a baseball game's seventh inning stretch. Late Chicago Cubs broadcaster Harry Caray began that Wrigley Field tradition. Lastly, ten die-hard Cub fans in 1966 began the famous Wrigley Field "Bleacher Bums" section. These lively fans have grown to become as much a part of Cubs baseball as the old-fashioned scoreboard and the ivy-covered walls.

The Chicago Cubs franchise enjoys an almost cult-like following. Fans flock to the rooftops of the buildings as well as the sidewalks and the streets that surround the stadium in all extremes of weather. They bring coolers; lawn chairs, portable radios and the occasional fishing net, harboring optimism that their stay on the roof might bring them a special treat – a home run ball hit by an up-and-coming rookie or a crafty Cub veteran. The fan following on Chicago's North Side has grown in such epic proportions that the Waveland, Addison, Sheffield, and Clark thoroughfares are more widely called Wrigleyville than their own given street names.

As a child, Kim had grown to love the middle of February because the Cubs' pitchers and catchers reported to Spring Training in Arizona at that time. Several of her parents' friends often commented that it was odd for a girl to recite the exact date and time that a baseball team's battery was due to arrive for pre-season practice, especially when Harold and Elizabeth's sons did not know.

As a result of her behavior, which her family and friends deemed quite uncharacteristic for a girl, one could have said that Kim was a tomboy. That would have been a fair assessment. If given the choice between wearing dresses and skirts or T-shirts and jeans, Kim always chose the latter. She seldom wore makeup. She lived what she described as "the simple life" and was very content to thrive within her own skin. Her family was not wealthy but raised Kim to appreciate the small achievements in life for their uniqueness and subtlety.

Growing up in a family of boys added to Kim's tomboy nature. Because she loved her brothers, she went everywhere with them. They never seemed to mind, either. Each boy believed that if their destination was not good enough for their sister, it was not good enough for them. Her parents raised their five children to honor that principle, second only to their faith.

Being a baby sister allowed Kim to develop a keen sense for the outdoors, but her competitive nature always led to a contest with the boys. It was obvious by the time she was nine that Kim had a natural gift for tossing a baseball. However, it was equally as true, yet not as widely known, that she was an avid fisherman.

As a toddler, Kim fished for muskellunge, northern pike, and catfish in the lakes of Minnesota. When her family moved to the Pittsburgh area, she frequented the banks of the Ohio, Allegheny, and Monongahela Rivers – the three famed rivers that are the namesake of the Pittsburgh Pirates' old Three Rivers Stadium. Those fishing trips, of course, led to the catching and releasing of many different varieties of river-based fish. The trips were also notorious for a game of baseball trivia.

Trivia had always played a prominent role in Kim's family. As a result of her father's years as a sportscaster and disc jockey, he had amassed a great knowledge base for everything surrounding the art of sports. Whether the tidbits were about records, uniform numbers, or the attendance at certain sporting events, Harold passed his awareness to his children in the form of trivia questions and meaningful discussions.

Harold, through years of disagreeing with his father over the White Sox–Cubs rivalry, always made sure he allowed his children to keep an open mind. He never forced his beliefs or comments upon the kids and wanted them to be independent. He wanted each child to be a sports fan, in some form. He just never saw his daughter as being the biggest baseball fan he knew.

While interested in all things baseball-related, Kim enjoyed Chicago Cubs baseball trivia and facts the most. She would regularly quiz her siblings on events that had occurred in certain games, in specific seasons, and on particular days.

For their children's Christmas in 1985, Harold and Elizabeth purchased a subscription to the Cubs' weekly *Vineline* publication, never envisioning that their teenage daughter would fight her brothers for the magazine with such frequency that the boys seldom had the chance to read it.

People who possess a genius for piano, writing, or dance fill this world; Kim's unique genius was baseball. Her divine love for the sport, its trivia, its history, and its symbolism set her apart from many girls but brought her much closer to her father.

When Kim was not wrangling with her brothers, she was more than likely found fishing with her father. Throughout history, statistics had proven that mothers and their sons usually bonded and so did fathers and their daughters. Kim had a close and fantastic relationship with both of her parents but held an inseparable bond with her dad. The conversations she had with Harold about baseball sounded more like two friends chatting about sports war stories than a father and daughter. Their discussions about the sport were rich and in-depth. And, at times, through Kim's love for research, she had even managed to stump her dad over certain aspects of baseball trivia. To say that Harold Reedeaux was proud of his daughter was not the proper observation. The word "proud" was simply not strong enough to emphasize his appreciation and admiration. She was growing up to be just like him.

The deepest bond between Kim and her father grew from their shared love for baseball and more specifically, Cubs baseball. Until he had attended the July 4, 1976, meeting between the Cubs and Mets in New York City, Harold had never witnessed a live Cubs game. Even after having attended the Bicentennial game in New York, Harold still had not experienced the aura that was and is Wrigley Field.

By the time he was nearly fifty years old Harold's dream of attending a Wrigley Field game was still left unfulfilled. He longed to smell the freshly cut Merion bluegrass and clover that covered the field. He yearned to enjoy the beauty of the two hundred Boston ivy plants that covered the stadium walls. His eyes ached to witness a Cub victory in a hard-fought, well-played game.

In light of his daughter's respect for the "greatest pastime on earth," Harold decided to take Kim to her first Cubs game.

Shortly after the moment when single game tickets for the Cubs season went on sale, late that February, Harold talked with a travel agent about the trip. Then, using some of his media connections at the *Chicago Tribune*, Harold secured the trip of a lifetime. He booked an early August vacation which allowed for one last father-daughter weekend before the start of the school year. The Cubs were scheduled to play the Montreal Expos, a team that was coming off a third place 1988 season that had seen 81 wins and 81 losses, a perfect .500 average.

As Kim prepared for the first season of her high school's new girls' baseball team, the Brentwood Lady Spartans, she struggled to stay focused. With every practice and every warm-up, her mind drifted to the sights and sounds that she would see and hear that August at Wrigley Field. In spite of her daydreaming, Kim knew she had a job to accomplish for the sake of her team. She was the captain of her Lady Spartans team. Because she had spearheaded the investigation into the school district's Title IX violations, Kim felt even more compelled to do well. Personally, she did not want her cause to be in vain, due to poor play.

Her play was far from substandard. In fact, Kim's play was better than most of her boys' baseball counterparts. She was solid in the shortstop position. She hit for a .406 average with one home run, fifteen RBIs and thirteen stolen bases. By season's end, her team captured their division's title and her coach selected Kim to play in the Western Pennsylvania Girls Baseball All-Star Game, the first contest of its kind.

After the historic Lady Spartans' season was complete, Kim was able to sit back and enjoy her main love in life – watching her beloved Chicago Cubs on TV. The high school baseball season had not finished until mid-May, when the Major League Baseball season had already been in full action for over a month.

The Cubs had come out of the gate in near mid-season form and in stellar fashion. The North Siders had started the season with a 1–2 record before reeling off seven straight wins. The team had faltered somewhat by the end of the month, finishing with a 12–11 record in April, but they showed a lot of heart and a lot of promise – just ask any Cub fan. Still, Cub fan or not, everyone knows that baseball seasons are not decided and World Championships are not won or lost based upon the happenings in the first month of the season.

Because Kim had followed the game from the time she was old enough to sit upright, she had developed a wonderful eye for talent. She also had an uncanny ability to predict how a season would end, just by what she had seen in the first few games in a season. After the month of April in 1989, Kim made a prediction that shocked her family, "The Cubs are going to finish in first place this year."

The prediction seemed sudden. Although the team, under the direction of a new club manager, had started strong, winning eight of their first ten games, on a seven-game road trip to Montreal and New York, the Cubs lost six of their next seven games. Completing April one game over .500 made the thought of winning the National League Eastern Division title seem unrealistic.

Kim was certain, however, and would not waver from her prophecy. As the summer months progressed and her vacation to Wrigley Field neared, the Cubs had looked as if they were falling apart more than they were coming together. In June 1989, the Cubs lost fifteen of their twenty-eight games. The team was still playing above .500 baseball but the media and fan outlook on the rest of the season was less than favorable.

The true Cub fans, such as Kim, defended their beloved ball club. They were a team of young men. That year, the average age of their starting team was 27.5 years – the age which most baseball experts consider to be a position ballplayer's "early prime." The average age of the pitching staff was 26.6 years, also representative of players just nearing their heyday. The team's youth spoke to how the players were still learning the game. Kim believed that to be a good indication for what the team would be able to accomplish.

Young people, especially athletes, are emotional by nature. They long to give their all for the sake of the team, but in doing so they often overlook their true potential. The veteran ball player who is team-oriented will leave everything on the field and be cautious, so as not to hurt the team; the rookie or inexperienced player will throw everything he feels he is capable of into the sport, for the sake of the team. That hard-nosed ideology can lead to careless errors that a seasoned veteran's patience would not permit.

The All-Star Break was fast-approaching for the four Cubs players named to the team. Kim believed that the All-Star appearance by those four players would energize the club as they began the second half of the season. Kim's prediction proved accurate.

The Cubs, three months later, became the champions of the National League's Eastern Division. However, the hearts and souls of Wrigleyville broke again when the San Francisco Giants ended the Cubs' miracle season by defeating them, four games to one, in the NLCS.

Afterwards, the media reports stated that the Cubs had been an "overachieving" team, worthy of their acclaim and yet a club destined for their ultimate demise. The comments regarding the Cubs' demise were in spite of their season record of ninety-three wins and sixty-nine losses. Kim and Harold were proud of the team's accomplishments, as were most Cub fans. One thing, however, was clear. For a chance at a World Series' berth, the story remained as it had been for forty-five years. On the North Side of Chicago, the common phrase was, yet again, "Wait Till Next Year."

CHAPTER 9

Jacques Barzun once wrote, "Whoever wants to know the heart and mind of America had better learn baseball, the rules and realities of the game – and do it by watching first some high school or small-town teams." There is an innate truth in this philosophy.

Major League Baseball, while the most widely known aspect of the game, does not tell the entire tale of the sport itself. Professional baseball has hills and valleys, if not entire territories, that are uncharted in the Little League, junior high, high school, and even college levels.

In Little League, the children play for the love of the game and for the discipline and enjoyment that the sport can provide. In junior high, the individual player's skill level is beginning to take hold and as the direct result of better play, the enjoyment factor is increased twenty-fold. By high school, many of the players have spent nearly half of their lives learning everything there is to know about the game and its rules. While the sport is still enjoyable during high school, the competitive nature and thrill in each victory tend to overshadow the bare fundamentals. At the college level, baseball is still an appreciated competition with emphasis placed on League Championships to bring added and needed revenue to the player's respective school. By college, if not before, the gifted athletes meet scouts for Major League franchises. The scouts chart each at-bat and monitor every ball, strike, pop-up, or home run and look for the one special player who will stand out, above and beyond the rest.

Once the athlete signs a Major League contract, emphasis on the almighty dollar takes on new meaning. Of course, there are exceptions to the rule, but the ad franchises in our country and around the world utilize the faces and talents of our professional athletes in all sports, not just baseball, for their own agendas. The ball player is paid well but somewhat used as a pawn for commercial advertising. Often times, the monetary gain afforded to professional athletes is worth more than the love of the game that had been present two decades before at the Little League level.

Such an event occurred to the Chicago Cubs organization after the All-Star break in 1989. Chris Blackmon was a twenty-two-year-old, left-handed pitcher from Missouri who had been a rookie in the Baltimore Orioles' organization the previous year. He came to the Cubs as a free-agent in the off-season and brought with him a mediocre arm and a hefty advertising scheme. Blackmon had secured advertising deals with everyone from soft drink companies to auto parts stores. He was swimming in endorsement dollars and seemed more interested in his own ego than any victories in the game at hand.

Blackmon, ineligible for the All-Star festivities, had pitched three innings of disastrous baseball in the Cubs' final outing prior to the All-Star break. He had allowed five runs on as many hits and left the game before the fourth inning of action had begun.

Instead of sitting with his teammates until the ballgame was finished, Chris Blackmon left the stadium and took a limousine to Chicago's O'Hare International Airport. He then boarded a chartered airplane for Dallas. He had prearranged the taping of five All-Star week advertisements for a regionally based airline and had agreed to visit the region's youth centers to talk with the kids about the game of baseball.

Chris filmed the ad campaign while standing on the top step of one of the airline's passenger jets. Three months beforehand, he had received a script to memorize for the piece. Incidentally, he missed five Cubs team practices as a result of that outside interest. (For what it is worth, I always wondered if he crammed too much jetlag into the space needed for simple tasks, like supporting the team.) A teleprompter had even been set, at the site of the filming, in the event that Chris would forget his lines. He did often.

On the day of the taping, intermittent showers added to the oppressive heat and humidity in the Dallas County area. The ad executives, in spite of the conditions, decided to go ahead with the filming, as had been planned. Chris climbed the airplane's stairs and turned as had been written in the script. Having forgotten his lines, he squinted and then leaned forward to see the teleprompter. When he shifted his weight forward, the moisture build-up on the airplane's stairs caused him to slide and he fell from the top step of the airplane. Unable to move, he was rushed to a hospital in Fort Worth where it was determined that Chris had torn the ACL and MCL in his left knee. The injury served to end his baseball season and, eventually, his career in the League.

Chris Blackmon's injury left the Cubs with a gap in the starting order. With a half season to go, the prospect of a four-man starting rotation was nothing that the front office, manager, pitching coach, or team wanted to entertain.

The Cubs organization placed a call to the team's AAA affiliate in Iowa and a pitcher named Leon Chapman arrived at Chicago's North Side with his ticket to the Big Show. Leon Chapman, yes, that Leon Chapman – the future strikeout king and Cy Young winner, the future shoe endorser extraordinaire and sure-fire first-ballot Hall-of-Famer. More importantly, he was the Leon Chapman who, in the World Series, nearing the end of his career over twenty years later would come face-to-face with a long-haired, nail polish–wearing ballplayer who had still been in high school during his 1989 rookie season.

Leon Chapman was born February 3, 1968, in a small white frame house on the outskirts of Beckley, West Virginia. His mother, Laura, had been a second grade teacher prior to the birth of her first child: Leon's older brother, Samuel. His father, Burl, was a coal miner who had come from a coal-mining family; Burl expected his sons to follow the family's tradition. The family of four lived a modest life until Burl developed black lung disease and passed away in 1970.

As the widowed mother of two small children, Laura returned to work in the Beckley school district until ovarian cancer claimed her life in 1972; two days shy of Leon's fourth birthday. Burl's parents, who lived in Charleston, West Virginia, took in the two orphaned boys.

The Chapmans were a practical coal-mining family. When the discussion arose about whether to buy new shoes or go out to a movie or a game, the shoes always won the argument. The state of West Virginia had no professional baseball teams and while it was only a four-hour drive from Charleston to Pittsburgh, Pennsylvania, home of the Pirates franchise, the trip would have never been cost- or time-effective. Every Sunday, Samuel and Leon invited their cousin, Rick, to play catch. Rick, seven years Leon's junior, looked up to Leon and enjoyed the time his cousin took to teach him about the game.

By the time Leon was in junior high, his grandparents' health had deteriorated to the point that they could no longer care for the boys. Leon and Samuel moved once again, this time to Boston, to live with their maternal grandfather. It was in Boston that Leon discovered a gift that would change his life forever – baseball.

Leon's grandfather, Les Hooper, had made a fine life for himself and their late grandmother, Gloria, working as a reporter for the *Boston Globe*, prior to his retirement in 1966. Les was a prominent member of the Boston community and still regarded as one of the region's most open-hearted citizens.

When Leon and Samuel were welcomed into their grandfather's large brick home on three fertile acres of lush green land, the boys had access to everything they could have imagined. The two-story, three-bedroom house was within walking distance of the local grocery store and eatery, while just a few miles from what was Leon's most coveted place, Fenway Park. It seemed that for two teenage boys, life could not have been better. But, then, Les handed the boys a "homecoming" gift: two tickets to the Red Sox Opening Day in Boston versus the Cleveland Indians.

Leon knew nothing about the Indians that year, nor did he care. He had the privilege of watching a live baseball game. That trip was not just a baseball game for the boys, though. For Samuel, the game meant the chance to see his hero, Carl Yastrzemski. For Leon, it meant the beginning of a thirty-plus-year affair with America's Favorite Pastime.

Scheduled for Monday, April 17th, the game featured less than ideal baseball weather. Marked by heavy cloud cover and a light mist in cool spring-like the air, the gloomy conditions seemed to make the "Green Monster" appear much larger, although the air smelled of freshly cut grass and hot dogs.

In spite of the clouds and mist, Samuel and Leon found their seats, perfectly centered along the first base side of the ballpark. Les had arrived at Fenway Park with his grandsons nearly two hours before game time and had thought that their early arrival would give him the chance to hold a meaningful conversation about the history of the game. Les's seemingly perfect plan did not proceed as intended. From the time that the three arrived to find their seats, Samuel and Leon had been in awe. As if the fact that they were sitting in a Major League stadium, and not just any Major League stadium – Fenway Park – had not been enough, the realization that their seats rendered a spectacular view of the left field fence, known as the "Green Monster," rendered the boys speechless. Their grandfather, trying to get three words from their mouths, said, "Bigger in person, ain't it?" All that Samuel and Leon could do was nod.

By game's end, most Boston fans were doing more than nodding; they were shaking their heads. The Cleveland Indians had stunned the

Red Sox by handing them a shutout. The Indians' crafty veteran pitcher had hurled nine innings of superb baseball and had only allowed two hits in Cleveland's 4–0 victory. However, the most important event of the day was uncovered as Leon and Samuel rode home with their grandfather. When Les asked his grandsons how they felt after the game, Samuel was saddened that his hero, Carl Yastrzemski, had gone hitless. Leon, however, was more upbeat and told his grandpa: "I am going to be a Boston Red Sox pitcher one day."

As a teenager, Leon was living the American dream and soon, thanks to a kind-hearted high school coach, Leon loved playing baseball. He continued to love the Red Sox and when he received word of an MLB tryout camp in Methuen, he went. The scouts called him a bona fide phenomenon, which later seemed to be the first step in the rise of his ego.

After a few years of working through the Minor League ranks, Leon was on a Major League baseball mound. It was not with the Red Sox, as he had hoped, but in 1989, at the age of twenty-one, Leon's perch atop the pitcher's mound at historic Wrigley Field was good enough for him.

Leon's first start as a Chicago Cub came on August 7, 1989. It was the first installment of a three-game series against the Montreal Expos. The Expos, which had seen a slow progression in the season turn into a team record of fifteen games over .500 by the first of August, were in the midst of a four-game losing streak when they arrived at the Friendly Confines for the three-game affair.

The rookie pitcher's first game also marked the first day of Kim and Harold Reedeaux's dream vacation to Wrigley Field. For Kim, the trip meant a chance to see her beloved Cubbies play live. For Harold, the trip meant a life-long dream fulfilled.

Harold and Kim's seats were just behind first base. The blazing hot late summer sun burned its way into Wrigley Field. The trademark winds from a nearby Lake Michigan were notably absent. Still, the oppressive heat did not matter. Harold and Kim were living their dream and nothing could have ruined their enjoyment.

Shortly before 1:20 p.m., the Cubs' outfield ran onto the grass and took their positions behind a visibly nervous Leon Chapman. That series held a greater interest to the Cubs organization since the Expos had swept their first meeting that June. The Expos' three-game sweep began a period where the Cubs lost seven of their next nine games. The stakes were high for some much deserved retribution. The team had veteran pitchers in line to start games two and three of the series. The Cubs' upper management felt that taking two of the three games would be a successful series.

While each game in a baseball season mattered, the beginning of August meant the beginning of "do or die" time for many teams. If the team played well, they would probably find themselves in the postseason. If the team faltered, even in the slightest sense, an early winter was a likely expectation.

Starting a rookie pitcher in a situation where the pennant race was tight and a victory in every game was a near necessity was a risky move but one in which the Cubs had no choice. So it was; with fresh-faced Leon Chapman on the mound, the first game of the Expos-Cubs series began. Twice in the first two innings, the Cubs' catcher had to go to the mound and work his motivational magic to calm the young recruit. It is during a time like this that the upper management in the organization feels incredibly fortunate to have a veteran catcher on their club.

The veteran catcher will try many techniques to calm a struggling pitcher. Sometimes, the motivation comes from past experience; other times, the catcher may resort to poetry or quotations that might help to alleviate the pitcher's duress. The pitcher needed such assistance for the situation that arose on August 7, 1989. It is one thing to pitch well in the Minors but with no pun intended, it is a whole new "ballgame" when a rookie makes his first appearance in "The Show." To the rookie pitcher, the adage that "first impressions are always the most remembered" is often hard to swallow. The rookie never intends to botch a play but on occasion, it is done out of nothing more than fear.

On that day, the catcher chose to recite a quote. The catcher did not say a word as he approached the mound. Leon, harboring a "deer in the headlights" look, feared being chastised for his performance. With an honest smile, normally covered by protective gear, the catcher looked into Leon's icy blue eyes and spoke a paraphrased quote by the great Nolan Ryan: "Your ability to throw a baseball is a gift. It is a God-given gift. It may take you some time to figure that out but once you do, you will dedicate yourself to becoming the best pitcher that you can be."

After that moment, Leon threw six straight strikes to get out of the inning. Nearly three hours later, Leon finished the ballgame, pitching a seven-hit complete game. More importantly, he had scored his first Major League victory when the Cubs won by the score of 5–2. Kim Reedeaux, who had caught a third inning pop-up from her seat along the first base line, ran down to field and yelled for Leon to come and sign her baseball. He looked at her with those icy blue eyes and said, "Go away, girl; I don't sign things for women." The Cubs went on to give the Expos a taste of their own medicine, sweeping the series in three straight games. All of Saturday and Sunday, Kim watched as Leon sat with the other pitchers, smiling a devilish and self-centered grin. "I wish I could fix him," Kim said to herself, still angered over his refusal to sign her baseball. "He needs an attitude adjustment."

The Cubs had traded Leon to Boston in the mid-1990s due to salary and interpersonal issues. Kim now found herself in a position to seize her chance at revenge.

In 1990, his first full year with the Cubs, Leon won sixteen games and was voted to his first All-Star team. Many fans said that his boyish charm granted him that honor, more so than his play. He was, after all, in his first full season and he did have an "eye candy" property about him. For television ratings' sake, the women were sure to watch, just to see him. His ability to charm, along with other things, had gone to his head. Within a year, he became a self-proclaimed "Ladies Man," but as the world would later learn, that was all a stunt; his opinion of women was clear and he was not discriminatory – he hated all women equally! Due to his attitude, ego, and demands, the Cubs' organization shipped Leon and some cash to the Red Sox in 1996 for two Single A–ball outfielders who never developed, just to free themselves of his headaches.

At the present moment, none of those things mattered. Leon was a Red Sox pitcher; Kim was the Cubs' batter, and they were one break in the clouds away from either reaping destiny or heartache.

CHAPTER 10

For a brief moment, the rain slackened and Kim decided to stroll from the dugout and wave to the cold and damp fans who braved the elements solely out of genuine respect for baseball and the chance to witness history. As she looked into the stands, she saw a little girl, no more than six or seven years of age. The girl had blonde hair, curled into tightly tangled ringlets, and glasses, which brought back a memory that Kim had promised she would never forget – Anna Merkel.

When Kim was a senior in high school, her baseball team was, again, a regional powerhouse. In two short years, they had become the envy of all high school teams, regardless of sport or gender. Each girl on the Brentwood Lady Spartans baseball team had a skill level above and beyond the expectations of high school athletics.

One bright and sunny mid-April day in 1990, the Lady Spartans were playing the Kings Branch Lady Knights. Kim batted second. To date, Monica Moreno, the Knights' pitcher, had held a perfect record for the season. She had no intention of letting Kim Reedeaux be the one to change that. With a runner on third in the bottom of the final inning, Kim was up to bat. She fouled the first pitch into the bleachers, and then crushed the second pitch to deep center field. The runner scored by sliding into home plate just as the catcher swiped, unsuccessfully, to tag. The Lady Spartans had won the game but the victory soon proved not the most important part of that game or even that day.

Kim looked into the bleachers as her teammates carried her off the field and saw a little girl who appeared to be around five years old clutching the foul ball that Kim had hit. The child was showing the ball to her mother and Kim smiled when she realized she had obviously made the girl's day. What Kim did not realize was that one foul ball would change the course of her life forever.

The Brentwood Spartans coaching staff invited the entire team to the local pizzeria for a post-game victory party. The game had been widely anticipated as being one that the Lady Spartans stood no chance of winning. In spite of the odds against it, Kim's solid fielding and her iron-clad strength had proven to be more than the entire Knights' shields and swords – or gloves – could defend. Kim sat in a booth in the back of the restaurant and began tearing away pieces of her pepperoni and mushroom pizza when she heard a little voice call her name. When she turned around, Kim saw the same little girl with the beautiful blonde ringlets who had so proudly waved around the foul ball Kim had hit into the stands during the sixth inning. "Hello, there," Kim said. "What is your name?"

"Anna Nicole Merkel," the little girl replied with a sense of certainty.

Kim introduced herself and then asked if Anna needed something.

"I am six," Anna said.

Kim acknowledged Anna's age and then noticed the baseball she held in her hand.

"What do you have?" Kim asked, already knowing the answer.

"This is yours," Anna replied. "Mommy said I should return things that are not mine."

Kim smiled and said that Anna had a good mommy. As Kim took the baseball from the little girl, Anna began to cry.

"Did you want to keep it, sweetie?" Kim asked. Anna nodded, wiping the tears from her eyes with her right hand, dirt-covered from the baseball.

"Do you like baseball?" Kim inquired.

"I like lots of things," Anna answered, before saying the one thing that had stayed in Kim Reedeaux's mind for nearly fifteen years.

"I have to like as many things as possible; the angels will be here soon."

"Angels?" Kim asked.

"Yes, the angels will come and carry me to my daddy," Anna announced. "That's what Mommy said."

"Why will the angels come, Anna?" Kim prodded, with a tear welling in her eye.

"I have cancer," Anna stated, with the strongest yet most innocent voice that anyone could have heard.

Kim reached into her purse, took out a pen, and not only gave the baseball to the girl, but signed it, too. Then Kim decided, without any reservation, that she would dedicate the rest of her season to Anna Merkel. She invited Anna to attend every game, through the end of the season and into the playoffs, agreeing to pay the admission for Anna and her family.

Nothing in Kim's life had been more moving than seeing the will and stamina that Anna showed, in spite of her obstacles. Kim, in a different yet similar way, was able to bond with the girl through a shared background of tough health situations. Outside of her family, Kim had never known anyone with whom she could discuss her own inauspicious life's beginning. No one ever fully understood what it meant to be so lucky and so blessed. Anna's fighting spirit was, indeed, contagious.

The last game of the season fell on a Thursday. The match-up was pivotal since the winner would emerge as the regular season league champion and have a first-week bye to start the playoffs. Anna had missed every contest for nearly three weeks due to treatment for her illness but her family made sure that she was present for that last game. What once seemed a simple act of kindness shared between a baseball player and a child had, by season's end, become a city-wide phenomenon. The entire Brentwood community had come to the stadium, not only to rally for their Lady Spartans but also to honor a selfless six-year-old.

As had been the case the day that her bond with Anna began, Kim came to the plate as the second batter in the bottom of the sixth inning. There were two runners on base, one at each corner. With two outs in a tied game, the outcome was riding on Kim's shoulders. She swung at the first pitch for a strike. She held off on the next, an outside curveball. The third pitch was a 71-mph fastball, waist high and right down the middle of the plate. Kim launched the ball from the stadium.

As she made her way around first base, Kim peered back in Anna's direction and smiled. Anna, though weak and pale, grinned back at Kim. The stillness in that brief moment reflected the kind of silence and subtle awe that come from viewing the fall foliage or a breathtaking sunset. The moment spoke volumes about the beauty of true and inseparable friendship. The approaching sunset that night looked to be beautiful, but Kim knew that Anna's last sunset was approaching. The thought weighed heavily on Kim's mind as she finished her victory lap.

When she touched home plate, Kim looked again in Anna's direction. She wanted to give Anna the bat used to hit the game-winning home run. But, as she gazed toward the first-base side of the stadium, she noticed that Anna and her family had already gone.

Kim, desperate to reach out to her brave, young friend, decided to forego the after-game pizza party. Instead, she signed the bat, loaded it into her truck, and drove to the wooded area on the outskirts of Brentwood where Anna and her family lived.

She arrived at the Merkel home just as the first stars appeared. Despite the hour growing late, the brilliant pink shading of the clouds and yellow-orange coloring to the spring sky gave the appearance of mid-day.

The Merkel family sedan was parked in the driveway of their frugal country cabin. Kim could not help but see that the cabin's roof needed some repair work; she figured that Anna's medical care had gone a long way towards draining the family's finances.

Just as Kim had begun to knock, Adolph Merkel, Anna's grandfather, appeared in the doorway. He invited Kim into the home and showed her the way to Anna's room. The inside of the cabin appeared much larger than it had seemed from the front. There were two long hallways: a main hall and another recessed one with a bedroom at each end. Anna's room was to the right. In the hallway, between the bedrooms, an antique cherry curio cabinet stood. The cabinet displayed porcelain dolls of different styles and sizes; Kim figured some of those had belonged to Anna's grandmother. The brilliant white hallway walls made the cabinet stand out even more. In the breezeway, where Kim entered the recessed hall and walked towards Anna's bedroom, was a small yet full bathroom with a fish theme. The soap holder, towels, and wallpaper were all of an aquatic nature. Given Kim's love of fishing, the décor made her smile.

Kim approached Anna's bedroom and brushed her hand along the beaded "Anna's Place" sign that hung on the door. The sign appeared as bright and precious as Anna. Just as Kim reached for the doorknob, Anna's mother, Sophie, came from the bathroom and expressed how her daughter had made the sign during a Bible Study outing when she was three years old.

When Kim entered the bedroom, she saw Anna, resting beneath three layers of Winnie-the-Pooh bedding. She looked cold and tired but appeared to be daydreaming about something.

"Anna, honey. Are you awake?" Kim asked, softly.

"Yes," Anna said, struggling for a word.

"I brought you this bat." Kim said, as she showed the little girl the metal Easton brand club she had used.

"Kim…" Anna started, "…will you win the playoffs for me?"

"I'll try my best," Kim said, as her friend's eyes closed. "I promise I'll try my best."

"Strike out every batter," Anna said, before falling asleep.

Kim stood by Anna's bed and smiled. She was her team's shortstop, not their pitcher. Kim did not figure that Anna really knew the difference. After all, she was trying to enjoy as many things as she possibly could in a short amount of time. Kim was sure that fighting cancer at such a young age was impossible enough to fathom.

For the rest of the evening, Kim thought of every way that she could to assist Anna in her final days. She wanted nothing more than to see that young girl's infectious smile at her playoff games. Sadly, that was not to be. Three hours after Kim had left the cabin, Anna died. Sophie called Kim the next morning to tell her.

At first, Kim was angry. After all, Kim had battled so hard to overcome her own childhood health obstacles that it did not seem fair that she lived so healthily, happily, and well, while others in the world suffered. Then, she remembered the playoffs and how Anna had made Kim promise to win the championship. From that moment on, Kim was determined.

The first playoff game was against Brentwood's archrivals, the Northgate Lady Flames. The Lady Flames had been a solid team in the previous year but had lost a good portion of their talent to graduation. About forty-five minutes before game time, Kim informed her coach that she wanted to pitch. Coach Gordon was one 100% against the idea. Strike that – he was 250% against the idea. He reminded Kim that the Lady Spartans were in the playoffs, which meant "win or wait till next year." Kim refused to budge, citing that she would either "pitch or sit out the entire game." The thought of losing the team's number one hitter, fielder, and scorer did not bode well for moving on to the second round of the playoffs. With Coach Gordon's hands tied, he allowed Kim to pitch, reasoning that the outcome of the game rested on Kim's shoulders. Kim was either going to prove herself as a brilliant decision-maker or a complete fool; either way, the future of her team's stay in the playoffs was her cross to bear. The answer to whether she was a genius or a fool would come later that night. Regardless, whether her team won or lost, Kim was going to pitch and intended to strike out every batter, just as Anna had requested.

That May day, the weather was had been unseasonably warm. By evening, the temperatures, still in the upper 70s, and the humidity level made the air heavy and stifling. Several fans waiting in line to enter the stadium commented that it was sure to rain. There was nary a cloud in the Western Pennsylvania sky that night.

The game began at 6:15, a little over four hours after Anna Merkel's memorial service at the Casella & Takeo Funeral Home. Kim had arrived at the stadium that night with a mascara-stained face and the black clothing she had worn to the funeral mass. To say that her emotions were running raw would have been an understatement. Still, Kim was determined to keep a promise to her late friend.

Brentwood's fans stood and cheered as their beloved Lady Spartans took the field. Then, several fans gasped when they saw Kim head to the mound. While Kim had played more than one position during her high school career, she had always been poised behind home plate as a catcher when she was not in the outfield. The fans were unaware of her pitching capabilities and her lightning-fast 70- to 75-mph fastball. The Spartans' faithful fans began booing Coach Gordon's decision; he looked at Kim and shrugged his shoulders. The fans' heckling only strengthened her determination and her goal to fan every batter.

Kim looked to the sky as she stood on the mound. She realized that, considering how energized as the fans were about the playoffs, her coach had set the world on her shoulders. Kim always tried to keep her promises, regardless of circumstances that might suggest they were unattainable. If Kim believed something was unattainable, she never promised it. As Kim bent to grab the baseball, she found the added strength she needed. The sun was setting for the day and early hints of nightfall had become visible. In the sky, hovering directly over Kim's head was one single star. Kim peered at the star for a moment and admired how it twinkled, just as Anna's spirit had twinkled each time they had been together. As the first batter for Northgate came to the plate, Kim glanced at her team's dugout and noted how her coach appeared nervous. His nerves seemed to match the butterflies in Kim's stomach.

The first batter was Dorothea Dixon, a six-foot, three-inch, mass of muscle. The newspaper rumored during the week preceding the game that Dorothea could bench-press over six hundred pounds and that she once changed the engine in her father's car, removing it unassisted. Dorothea's size did not intimidate Kim; neither did the fact that she had hit twenty home runs in the regular season. Dorothea stared into Kim's bright eyes and proceeded to watch three straight fastballs whiz by her for the first out of the game. The at-bat had been the first of the game but by game's end, the story remained the same.

Kim was unsuccessful in "striking out every batter" per se. But she threw a "no-hitter," striking out ten batters over six innings, as her Lady Spartans team defeated the Northgate Lady Flames by a score of 8–0. After the game, when Kim looked to the sky yet again, she noticed that the lone star in the sky had remained directly above her head the entire night. As Kim began to look away, the star twinkled. She suspected the star had been Anna, smiling down and then winking, giving her seal of approval.

Kim, during her final season as a member of the Brentwood Lady Spartans team, had helped to lead her team to their first Pennsylvania State Championship. In the championship meeting against the Seton-LaSalle Lady Rebels, Kim hit for two doubles and one home run; the Lady Spartans went on to win the State Title, 14–4.

After the game, Kim was met by Sophie Merkel, Anna's mother, in the locker room. Sophie had attended the game to support the team but more so, to show her appreciation for Kim's gesture of kindness throughout Anna's final months of life. At that meeting, Sophie presented Kim with a locket. The round, engraved silver locket had Anna's picture inside and an inscription on the back by Pastor, Rick Warren, which read: "Where your dreams are concerned, be careful not to sell yourself short. Dream a large dream – and then spend the rest of your life making it come true." The inscription made Kim cry, at first. After all, Anna died at age six and her dreams never had the chance of fulfillment. As she mulled over the verse's meaning, however, Kim made the decision that would forever change her life. She had always dreamed of becoming the first female professional Major League Baseball player and through the courage of one precious angel, Kim decided she would make that dream come true.

Years later, the rain in Chicago had begun to pick up in intensity again. Kim was still standing on the field, near the Cubs' dugout, admiring the daring and die-hard fans as they braved the elements for the sake of their team and the hope that day would end with their team's long-awaited World Series title. Kim's eyes, however much they gazed across the stands, always returned to the little blonde-headed girl with ringlets who reminded her so much of Anna.

Kim, visibly upset from thinking of Anna, went back into the dugout at the urging of her teammates. After she sat for a minute or two, she called for an usher. When Wilson Roberts, a twenty-year

Wrigley Field veteran, arrived, Kim walked onto the field with him, pointed to the little blonde in the stands, and handed him a signed baseball to give to the girl.

As she walked away, Kim muttered to herself: "This is for you, Anna; this one's for you."

CHAPTER 11

The least kept secret in human culture is that life is not always easy. Every day, someone will find that each road they travel may be smoother or rougher than another one. One person's smooth road may be a hard road to bear for someone else. The reasoning makes limited sense but that is life, plain and simple.

In 1991, Kim Reedeaux was a nineteen-year-old shortstop and pitcher who had graduated from high school the previous summer. She left Pennsylvania, two months after finishing school, to pursue the "opportunities that Chicago, Illinois had to offer." At least that is what she told her parents. In reality, she was in the Lake Michigan region to pursue her baseball aspirations. She had leased a small apartment in the Chicago suburb of Oak Brook and enjoyed the closeness to her favorite baseball team, the Cubs.

On her first Saturday night in Cook County, Illinois, Kim drove into Chicago and then, took the subway to West Kenzie Street where she ate in style at Harry Caray's famed Italian restaurant. It was while staring at a picture of the Cubs' broadcasting icon that Kim developed a plan for pursuing her baseball dreams.

Because of her father's sports influence – over three decades of work in sports and talk radio – Kim had some background knowledge into how the scouting system worked. She knew that each Major League team and the Major League Scouting Bureau held yearly tryout camps searching for prospective players. Kim also knew that every scout used a scale to rate the talent of every individual. Kim's plan was to contact the Major League Scouting Bureau Office and request information about when and where their tryouts would occur. Once she had uncovered a tryout date, Kim planned to fly home and with the help of her high school baseball coach and family, show her skill level on videotape. With her plan in place, Kim was in a good mood. That is, until she looked up from devouring the last bite of her chicken Caesar salad to see someone she had not seen in over a year, Cubs' pitcher Leon Chapman.

Kim tried not to stare at Leon and yet, she could not help it. Leon had a presence – a penetrating presence – which could pierce through even the most callous of people. His icy blue eyes stood out like aquamarine gemstones and sparkled every time he laughed. As charming as he was in appearance, it was no wonder that everyone became quieter when he entered a room. Yet, his personality seemed at odds with the appearance he portrayed.

Over the past season, the media had begun to cover various stories of how Leon paid no respect to women. The media's treatment of the story became more intense after a Major League study had proven that women, by a three-to-one margin were, indeed, avid baseball fans. The Commissioner's report, joined with the survey findings, led to the creation of a task force with the lone purpose of developing better ways to serve the needs of the female baseball fan.

Leon had publicly gone on record, shortly after the findings of the survey were released, to say that baseball was - without a doubt - a man's sport and that there was no place for a female team owner, bench coach, manager, or player in the game. Heck, Leon did not even feel there was any place for a female baseball fan. He had started a "Bags for Stags" campaign with the hope that men, nationwide, would support his cause and crusade against the role of women in any baseball capacity.

Harold Reedeaux had flown to Chicago, earlier that year, to interview Leon in regards to his anti-women-in-baseball campaign. He asked Leon about his dislike for women and Leon's response was one not repeatable in many circuits, except for possibly late-night cable television. Leon hated women; that was clear. No one, however, seemed to understand why. Of course, there were rumors and many of those speculations were lewd, crude, and borderline slanderous.

The *Gossip Zone* publication alleged Leon's involvement in fifteen felonious assault and sexual harassment cases against his former girlfriends. He denied the claims as unfounded, but court documents of public record don't lie, even if no jail record was ever uncovered. He sued the magazine for slander but after the periodical refused to settle, Leon withdrew his case, fearing he would come before a predominantly female judge and jury. The story did not end when the case did. Every media outlet in the country began covering the story of Leon's liaisons and bigotry. The headlines ranged from "Leon Chapman: Male Freak" to "Major League Baseball: Male Room Only." Still, in spite of the rumors and suggestions, no one in media had managed to uncover the true reason why Leon despised women. That is, no one uncovered Leon's secret until Timmy Coronado came along.

Timmy Coronado was twelve years old. As a sixth grader, he had won an essay competition that a popular children's magazine had hosted. The prize was a one-year reporting internship for the magazine as the publication's official "kid correspondent." The young reporter loved baseball, so when his summer vacation from school arrived and he was offered the chance to leave his home in the Cleveland, Ohio, to cover an August Cubs' series, he jumped at the opportunity. While Timmy was a small, freckled, red-headed boy who many of his classmates had viewed as the "Teacher's Pet," he had a natural ability when it came to reporting. He knew what questions to ask. Timmy never feared asking the questions that others avoided; he armed himself with a back-up plan, should anything in his approach go awry. Deep in his heart, he wanted to become the next Ty Cobb, but a journalism career seemed more likely.

Timmy arrived in Chicago three weeks after the 1990 All-Star Break. He had one goal in mind for his journey; he was going to get to the bottom of the "gender-bashing" issue surrounding Leon Chapman. In keen journalistic fashion, Timmy devised an outline for approaching the interview. First, he had planned to contact the organization to obtain the information for Leon's agent. Then, he would ask the agent's permission for the interview. With granted permission, a time for the interview was set and the meeting scheduled. To a twelve-year-old, the outline sounded like a good idea and one easily accomplished in one weekend. But, Major League Baseball had other ideas.

Timmy called the Cubs' front office and spoke to the General Manager's secretary. She had stated that GM Harry Friedman would return his call. The Cubs-Cardinals series passed. Timmy returned to the Cleveland metro area without the interview he longed to conduct. Timmy – the kid – had enjoyed the trip but Timmy – the reporter – wanted answers. From his home in Mentor, Ohio, Timmy contacted the front office again. He did so, twice a week, for the next five weeks. After receiving no assistance, he contacted the *Chicago Tribune.*

The Tribune Company, then sole owner of both Wrigley Field and the Chicago Cubs organization, had enjoyed an onslaught of fan support since the early 1980s. During just the 1989 season, the little ballpark on Chicago's North Side had entertained 2,491,942 fans, many of whom were women. The allegation that Leon Chapman had spoken against the female gender's involvement as fans of the time-honored tradition known as baseball was one that the corporation took seriously. It had never been, and it would never be, the opinion of a baseball team's – any baseball team's – ownership that one group of citizens would be hailed above and beyond another.

The department heads at the Tribune Company assured Timmy that a full investigation would take place. It did not take long for the inquiry to begin. Within a week, the front of the newspaper and the entire sports section buzzed with everything from photos to columns in regards to Leon Chapman's behavior. By the end of the next week, nearly three-quarters of the newspaper's 2.5 million readers called the Cubs' front office, complaining about Chapman's conduct and demanding some recourse by the team.

Faced with accepting either a full season's suspension from baseball or granting a sit-down interview to come clean about his ill-regard toward women, Leon agreed to accept the interview and assured the team that he would answer each question, truthfully. When the Tribune Company – citing bias toward their conducting of the interview – chose to fly little Timmy Coronado back to Chicago to carry out the meeting, everyone seemed surprised, including the twelve-year-old and his family. The Tribune Company made sure all of the arrangements were made. Timmy and his family flew, first-class, from Cleveland to Chicago, were housed in a five-star hotel near Lake Michigan, and enjoyed a private conference room at the WGN studios. The young journalist-to-be came prepared with everything he needed for his story. Armed with the questions he had written months before, Timmy sat in an overstuffed black leather swivel chair and awaited Leon's arrival.

Uncharacteristically, Leon arrived for the meeting fifteen minutes ahead of schedule. While he had brought his attorney and agent along to witness the proceedings, Leon had signed an affidavit that stated he would answer each of Timmy's questions truthfully and efficiently.

Timmy started the interview with some non-scandalous and general topics concerning baseball and his career choice. Then he asked the bombshell: "Mr. Chapman, why are you anti-woman?" Leon's answer brought a sense of astonishment to everyone in attendance. "All the women in my life have left me."

Leon Chapman was twenty-three years old; yet, in somewhat of a juvenile fashion, he subconsciously blamed his mother's death on her "abandonment" of him, instead of God's will. In the interview, Leon confided that having lost his father at a young age, he had depended on his mother as his supporter. He went on to confess that when she died, he felt alone and though he had lived a wonderful life, filled with more than he could have ever envisioned, the void his mother's death left was one that neither time – nor woman – could heal. Women served as a painful reminder of an irreparable hole in his heart; thus every relationship he had known ended in failure, further adding to his grief. Once Timmy published his guest article in the *Tribune*, Leon's testament read as though he had led a rough life, worthy of some sympathy. Was Leon a damaged man or someone using another ploy for media attention? Time would tell.

After the interview printed, Leon issued a public apology to every woman in the Chicago area and all women Cubs fans' worldwide. He confessed that he had been bitter and wrong for a long time and that the persistence of a twelve-year-old boy's interest in his story had inspired him to change. Shortly thereafter, elderly women from all over the Chicago area were offering to "adopt" Leon as their own child; younger women were offering to date or marry him. Life returned to normal. Leon gave no more public statements regarding his dislike of women and no one mentioned it in their daily discussions any longer.

Still, deep within Leon Chapman was ire. The rage that Leon possessed in his heart was a fury that was certain to one day burn out of control. When the stakes are high, one often finds it easy to say whatever one feels will alleviate a situation so it will disappear. Even though the pressured person knows it is wrong to speak less than the truth, many people find it easier to remove their lives from the truth than to face it, head first. That is exactly what Leon Chapman had done during his interview with Timmy. He had stated exactly what the Chicago Cubs organization, the Tribune Company, and the women in the Windy City area had wanted to hear. He did so merely to save himself.

Leon Chapman was not a changed man. He had used his bosses, the ball club, his community, and the legions of Cub fans as pawns in an elaborate lie that everyone in the world believed. Everyone, that is, except Kim Reedeaux and her family.

Kim tried not to focus on Leon; there were many other patrons at the famed dining establishment. Yet, she kept returning to Leon. He was a man of poor taste and poorer character. As he sat at a table across the bar from where Kim was dining, Leon seemed anxious. He seemed to sense that someone was watching him. He rose from his seat, turned around, and looked directly at Kim. Over the course of the past year, he had seen millions of Cub fans pack the stadium and yet he remembered her. There was something about Kim that did not sit well. He could not determine a reason but he knew there was something about her that he did not like, aside from the obvious fact she was female.

Just as Leon began walking in Kim's direction, a young woman, approximately twenty years of age, approached him. Kim overheard the conversation as the woman asked for his autograph. Leon's response to her: "I don't sign my name for any woman!"

Leon's attitude at the restaurant had served to strengthen Kim's resolve and opinion of Mr. Chapman. She left the restaurant with a renewed sense of purpose as she prepared to embark upon proving herself as a genuine baseball prodigy. She knew the path consisted of uncharted territory and that she would find many bumps along the way. Yet, after seeing Leon Chapman's behavior that night, she was more determined than ever to reach her dream. She set aside the next Monday as day one in her quest for the Big Leagues.

Kim awoke before daylight that early Monday morning in August. She had decided to start small and dream big as she began researching Major League tryout camp possibilities. Since she had always been a Cub fan, Kim decided to contact the Cubs' Front Office to inquire about their tryout schedule. The secretary was more than happy to share the information. Kim, not wanting to show her hand too quickly, left the secretary with the impression that she was getting the details for a male relative or friend. The plan would have worked, had the secretary not been an inquiring kind, who said, "So, what position does your brother or cousin play?" Honest with the secretary, Kim confided that she wanted the information for her own aspirations. The secretary nearly laughed and she was not the only one to find Kim's ambition funny.

The next twenty-five contacts that Kim made harbored the same opinion as the Cubs' office secretary. A girl wanting to try out for Professional Baseball seemed as ludicrous as a walking a batter with the bases loaded; it was something that just should not happen. Some contacts cited the 1952 ruling that prohibited women in professional baseball; other contacts said that Kim should consider some other means of being involved in the sport. None agreed that a women trying out for a Major League Baseball team was a good idea and henceforth, no one would give her the information she needed.

Kim knew that her videotape plan would never be a feasible option. After all, if the secretaries would not talk with her, the scouts were certain to disregard a female on a videotape. This knowledge led Kim to do something still discussed to this day. She knew that the Cubs held tryout camps in Illinois, so she contacted her older brother in Pennsylvania, had him call the Cubs' front office and state that his name was Kim. Within a half an hour after that call, Kim – the girl destined to "work in the kitchen," as one baseball executive had said – held the Cubs' upcoming tryout information in the palm of her hand. She had only a week to prepare for the outing.

The mid-August tryout camp would happen at a community college in Joliet, Illinois. Kim had spent the six days between learning of the camp and tryout day cleaning and re-lacing her glove and practicing her 60-yard dash speeds. She had requested and received the necessary release form from her father, stating that the ball club would not be responsible for any injuries and Kim felt that she was ready for the challenge. The camp had a 10 a.m. start time that morning with registration slated to begin at 9:30. Kim arrived by 8:45 but before she had left her apartment, she had pinned her hair under her baseball cap. The young ballplayer figured any angle she could gain on the scouts would be a point in her favor.

By the 9:30 registration time, nearly 175 men had shown for the camp; Kim was the only woman and at that time, no one had seemed to notice her gender. After all, how many women appear at tryout camps dressed to play? If anyone noticed her, they probably assumed she was just a somewhat effeminate-looking guy. With so many applicants to process, Kim had been able to fill out her registration form without any questions from the staff. The field was buzzing with excitement and action; no one noticed "the girl." The scouts and their assistants looked at the forms, but apparently assumed that "Kim" was just another one of the guys. In Kim Reedeaux's mind, she was. She was as much a baseball player as the next person on the field.

It was a long, hot, nerve-exhausting day, as the warm morning sun quickly became a sweltering afternoon heat wave. The weather forecast predicted the hottest weather of the summer season and Kim was beginning to believe it, as she sat and waited for her chance to shine. Even with the large number of camp participants, the thought was in the back of her mind that someone had noticed her gender and was therefore, made her suffer by making her wait. Others that had signed in for the camp after Kim arrived had proven themselves, while she still waited. She sat alone and wondered if the scouts were hoping that she would leave. She was a woman, after all; everyone knew she was wasting her time, or maybe not. As the sun peeked behind the one cloud in the late afternoon sky, Kim heard the words she had been longing to hear: "Reedeaux, are you ready?" Kim didn't say a word; she just grabbed her glove and ran.

CHAPTER 12

Some of the best moments in our lives come unexpectedly or seem unplanned, even if spiritual beings know that their chosen god plans everything. Whether we are discussing a rain shower that comes on a sweltering mid-summer afternoon or a wild pitch in the bottom of the ninth inning that allows the winning run to score, there is a keen appreciation for the things in life that come to us without cause or reason.

On that mid-August afternoon in 1991, two scouts from the Chicago Cubs organization discovered one such unexpected gift. The team had gone from winning the N.L. East pennant the year before to a season filled with scandal, injuries, and a below .500 standing. If there was one thing that was apparent, the team needed an edge. Everyone from the management to the scouts to the fans knew it; something had to change. From the managerial standpoint, there were questions as to how something could go from so right to so wrong in so short a time span. The fans echoed management's questions. The diehard team cheerleaders did not care how the problems resolved; the ultimate fan's mindset was "Just win!"

For Kim's first tryout feat, she ran the 60-yard dash, a requirement for all prospective Major Leaguers. A good time in the sprint was something in the 6.5 to 6.8 second range; Kim's time was a lightning fast 5.79. Next, Kim threw a series of pitches. First, she hurled a fastball, then a curveball, and next a slider. After the fastball flew to home plate at a speed of 93 miles per hour, the scouts asked to see a second fastball. The second pitch was 96 miles per hour. Kim continued to throw and by the time the scouts had seen enough, she had tossed 10 fastballs, all in the 92- to 97-mph range. The scouts called her over to a table where they could discuss things.

The first scout introduced himself as Don Golan. He was a tall, sleek-looking man who had an obvious baseball background. He seemed to be very knowledgeable and wise when it came to his expectations of the camp's participants. The second scout, Earl Mueller, had an obvious chip on his shoulder. His wry attitude was more prominent than his beer belly, graying moustache, and red sideburns. Early that morning, Kim had sensed that if she had a chance to impress the scouts, she needed to get through to Mr. Golan. It was not very long, however, before Kim realized she had a problem – the scouts that watched from a distance believed she was a boy.

"Son," Don began, "you have a fireball for an arm, you know that?" Kim did not know what to say. She knew the minute she opened her mouth that the scouts would know that she was female. Yet, she also knew that if her dream was to become reality, she would have to face them.

"Yes, sir," Kim said confidently. The scouts, having looked away for a moment, quickly turned toward her again once they heard her voice. Before Kim had a chance to say anything else, Don gave her a glimmer of hope.

"Well, a girl," Don stated. "In my eyes, gender doesn't matter; you still have an…" Don's colleague cut his sentence short and asked to speak with him in private. Kim smiled as the two began walking away from her.

"We cannot judge the talent of a girl; the law says we can't," Earl explained as he walked with Don toward the pine trees that surrounded the baseball diamond. "Girls are not allowed in pro baseball – that's that." Don knew that but he also knew that most girls did not carry the skill level that Kim possessed or showed them.

"Every rule can be overlooked, can it not?" Don asked as Earl eyed him with a look of extreme doubt. History has shown the professional baseball player in violation of the rules on numerous occasions. Hitters have utilized corked bats for added power at the plate; pitchers have used everything from spit to tobacco juice on the ball to change the arc and velocity, and players have used various steroids to bulk their bodies, in the belief that doing so would enable greater power. The violations that occurred throughout history – while wrong and not condoned – made the fact that Kim was, in fact, a girl, rather moot to Golan.

The game is not without its flaws. Players test the rules more frequently than in the past. Is this right? No. But, the business of professional sports has grown to generate such revenue for both the franchise and the individual player that a "win at all costs" ideal is often the most popular to pursue.

"What about the 1952 law?" Earl asked.

"What about it?" Don replied. "Laws can change." Mr. Golan was correct in his premise; baseball laws could change and, in fact, had changed.

Over the century that baseball has been a competitive sport, several challenges of its laws and regulations have taken place. Some challenges to baseball law, while unsuccessful, had ultimately led to needed change. In 1970, centerfielder Curt Flood, filed a lawsuit in which he challenged Major League Baseball's reserve clause. The clause had held that a player belonged solely to the team which held his contract, meant that the individual athlete was essentially "bound" by the organization that paid him. The policy left no leeway for the ballplayer to influence his own destiny.

The New York Federal Court heard Flood's case and decided the complaint held no merit. Still, the Federal Court Judge that oversaw the hearing suggested reserve system changes be implemented. Within the next few years, the judge's suggestion came to the forefront of baseball negotiations and by the end of the 1972 baseball season; Major League Baseball's owners ceased the reserve clause after agreeing to salary arbitration.

Of course, there was an apparent difference between the enacted salary arbitration policies and the law that banned women from participating in professional baseball. Yet, baseball's past legal rulings had proven its strongholds to be fallible.

Anyone who knew the slightest bit of information about the sport and its laws was aware that change, while not easy, was indeed, possible. Kim had held that rationale close to her heart for years and though Don Golan was a scout who normally chose the "by the book" approach, he had quickly come to realize that some people are natural-born athletes. He understood that punishing these athletes' for their talent, due to disagreements or gender, was unnecessary.

Earl continued to state his point about women, baseball, and how the two did not – and should not – mix. Don, however, had stopped listening. His eyes fixated on Kim Reedeaux. She was well-spoken, warm spirited, confident, and destined for greatness. If any other woman had come up against Earl's criticism, Don knew that woman would have walked away and written off her dream something crazy, just as Earl had noted. Not Kim, though. She sat on the grass despite the hot, afternoon sun and waited for whatever verdict was destined to come. She was still proud of her efforts for the day and was not about to let any shortfall at this first tryout camp disturb her. That positive attitude was why, in spite of the odds against her or opinions about her, Don decided he was going to help this athlete in her attempt to reach her dream.

Evening neared and the sun began to lose some of its grip on the Illinois skyline. With Earl still pacing back and forth beneath the conifers, Don strolled back to the field to find Kim seated quietly where he had left her nearly an hour earlier.

"Ms. Reedeaux," Don began "my partner and I have discussed your ability and have decided that you are not suited well enough for what this club deserves." Kim began to apologize for wasting the scouts' time when Don continued, his hand up to his mouth as to share an intimate secret. "You're too good for this team."

"Excuse me?" an exasperated Kim exclaimed.

"You're too good," Don repeated. "We travel to many cities and see many ballplayers over the course of the year. You have an amazing ability, unlike what we have seen in our male athletes this year. The Cubs are down and look to be down for some time; I believe you should look for other baseball avenues more suited for your talent level."

With that statement, Don gave Kim his business card and told her to refer any questions she had or comments she chose to make to his office.

"What about Mr. Mueller?" Kim asked. "Did he have a change of heart about me?"

Don lifted his finger to his mouth, looked toward Kim and said, "Baseball lesson number one: Never question a gift." Then, he went on to explain Earl's situation.

The only son of Heinrich and Henrietta Mueller, Earl spent his tender years in The Bronx. In the late 1930s, Heinrich was a railroad worker along the Hudson River. When the Second World War beckoned, he traveled to the Pacific and saw combat action in the historic battles of Midway and Guadalcanal.

When Heinrich returned from the War, everything that the Mueller family had known changed significantly. The long discussions the family once had about life – and all things good about it – ceased; the musical sounds of Billie Holiday and Glenn Miller that had once filled the family room had been quieted; and most noticeably, the joy that Heinrich had once found from sharing the love of baseball with his son had fallen so far from view that it was never illuminated again.

When Earl reached young adulthood, he had wanted to play for his high school's newly formed baseball team; Heinrich refused to allow it, citing that baseball was a game of dreams and that this world was far too serious for silly-hearts and foolishness. By that time, Heinrich's bitterness had taken control of the Mueller household and irreversibly changed each member of the family. Earl longed for his father's acceptance and approval; therefore, he forewent his baseball goals.

In the wake of World War II, Earl had so desperately sought his father's acceptance that he had forever changed life as he had once known it. As a result of needing Heinrich's support, Earl chose to sacrifice his idolization of the simple game of balls and strikes he had known as a child for the sake of following sports such as tennis and golf, the only two "genuine" sports the elder Mueller accepted in the post–World War II era.

When his father passed in 1974, Earl knew what he had to do. His eternal love for baseball remained. While aware that he was too old to become a baseball player, he chose to embrace his life-long bond with the sport in another way. In the summer of 1975, Earl quit his job in Manhattan to pursue his own dream of becoming a professional baseball scout. Earl realized the importance of locating quality talent so that baseball's enjoyment could continue for years, decades, and centuries to come. Earl wanted to play a small part in baseball's success and leave his own mark on the popularity of the game.

The road to becoming a baseball scout is just as lengthy as the path for those wishing to play the game. Most professional baseball scouts enter the realm by having participated in the sport as players. Others have held long-standing careers as high school or college coaches. The key element to scouting is an obvious eye for talent – or lack thereof. Earl Mueller's only experience was coaching the local high school's girls' softball league. His Major League scouting dream appeared to be far-fetched, at best.

He knew the talent level of the girls in the softball league but baseball and boys' sports were a much different process. The dissimilarities between the two superseded the likenesses. Still, Earl held a personal trump card. Life may not always be easy but one thing is clear, winners tend to find ways of getting things accomplished. Earl Mueller was a winner.

In 1977, Earl's seventh season as head coach of the Malarkey High School Lady Mustangs, his team was a perfect 20–0 and headed for the state playoffs. Earl was proud of his team but more so of the fact that he saw the potential to reach his own personal goal. With the 1975 advent of the International Women's Professional Softball League (IWPSA), Earl knew that if his girls could secure the state title, many of them would likely find success through college softball scholarships. Furthermore, he envisioned many more of his girls achieving success in a professional softball league. He knew if the softball scouts attending the game would view the girls' play; it would improve their chances for continued greatness.

The game was scheduled for 7:30 and the crowds were quite raucous. Earl's Lady Mustangs were set to face their toughest challenge of the year, a showdown with the Albany Catholic Academy's Lady Albatrosses. Albany was also undefeated and their pitcher, Nicole Albemarle, during her freshman year of high school, had signed a letter of intent to play college softball at Southern Cal. The game was certain to be a hard-fought battle, a contest between the best of the best, with the 1977 New York State Softball Championship as the prize to the winner. All Earl needed his girls to do was win the game.

Halfway through the six-inning contest, the Mustangs were up by three runs. A victory for Earl's team looked to be a lock. Amber Bennavito, Malarkey's star pitcher, had been nearly perfect. She had walked one batter in the first inning but had fanned every other girl she had faced.

Albany's star hurler had been removed from the game in the second inning due to a strained calf muscle and had been replaced by five-foot, two-inch, Jessica Mendez. Jessica, a senior, had not pitched a game for the Albatrosses all season. Due to her petite size and surgically repaired knee, she realized that her softball career was over before it really began. She found pride throughout the season in her new role as a benchwarmer, happy to support her team. Yet, with her team's resources exhausted, Jessica's coach had no other option than to place her on the mound.

When Earl received word that Jessica was entering the game for Albany, he silently applauded. In Earl's eyes, Jessica was a broken-down high school ballplayer placed in a situation that her coaches knew was a mistake. Earl saw the decision as a desperation measure, surely to backfire and bode well for his girls. But the one thing that Earl had forgotten is that there are two sides to every story. Yes, Jessica had not faced a batter in nearly two seasons, and yes, she was coming into the biggest game of her life seemingly unprepared for the task ahead;

however, Malarkey was not prepared for Jessica, either. They knew not of her abilities, her finesse, her candor, or her confidence.

Jessica's first inning of work for Albany had produced the three Malarkey runs. Afterwards, she was untouchable and in the bottom of the sixth, with the bases loaded, Jessica hit a grand slam homer over the right field fence to defeat Earl's Lady Mustangs 4–3, winning the state title for her team.

From that point forward, Earl Mueller held a true disrespect for women who opted to participate in a sport, regardless of the level. Instead of taking the defeat as "just a part of the game" or realizing that Albany's team had been better that day, Earl chose to chastise his girls, stating in the media and elsewhere that "they had let him down, uncommitted to the game."

Earl took a boys' baseball coach position the next year and held that role for nearly five more seasons. In those years, he sent twelve of his baseball players to the college ranks. Then, in 1982, he finally found his calling as a professional baseball scout. Yet, eight years into his scouting career, he still blamed his 1977 girls' softball team for "holding back his dream." So, when Kim Reedeaux arrived at the Cubs' baseball camp that mid-August day, Earl was against her from the moment he learned her gender. It was obvious that a law change would have to take effect before Earl would accept the fact that Kim had talent. Even then, within his heart, he would never "accept" Kim's ability, even if forced to abide by it.

All opposing opinions aside, Kim had completed the first leg of her journey. She had succeeded in performing well at a Major League Tryout Camp and had made a new friend in pro scout Don Golan. After all, former Major League pitcher Jim Abbott, had said it best: "Find something you love, and go after it, with all of your heart." That was exactly what Kim Reedeaux was doing.

CHAPTER 13

At the beginning of the 1992 season, the Chicago Cubs' organization was at a crossroads. Three years removed from their overwhelming success, something that had sparked high expectations for finally ending the "curse" that many had believed befell them, the team had begun the season with a 7–13 record in April. Everyone seemed tired. The team looked ragged, management appeared tired, and moreover, the fans were rapidly growing weary of the "loveable losers" mantra that had become their beloved ball club's theme.

Charlie Dirges, a former Major League player and longtime baseball executive, came to Chicago after the 1991 season to serve as the team's new general manager. Like all new hires in professional sports – especially for a team in such a World Series drought – Charlie's first public interview contained flowery words of promise and change. Dirges had assured the fans in attendance at the Wrigley Field press conference, and those worldwide, that the start of the 1992 season would bring the club's "best start in fifty years." By the end of April, disgruntled fans were illuminating the phone lines of WGN-Radio asking the commentators, or anyone who would listen, if Dirges' next promise would be selling the fans on a bridge in the middle of the Arizona desert.

Society, at the beginning of 1992, had begun a period that would become more and more fast-paced as the years progressed. The adage of "good things come to those who wait," was quickly being surpassed by the fact that every want and need was and/or would soon be at one's fingertips by clicking a few keys at one's desktop, thanks to the advent of the internet. Despite the advances, however, some things were still out of technology's control. The internet still could not turn the Cubs into winners, though I am sure a few fans probably tried to find a way. Technology was not able to perfect the weather so that the opposing team's long fly-balls stayed in the ballpark; they still sailed on the strong, Lake Michigan-based winds to the pavement on Waveland Avenue.

Likewise, these tools were not able to calculate whether a called strike three was indeed, ball four. Human error was and will always play a vital role in the success or demise of any ball club.

Charlie Dirges knew that with fan support faltering and team support wavering, he had to devise a plan for the future that would be entertaining and profitable. In 1991, Charlie had read about Kim Reedeaux in the *Charleston Daily Mail* newspaper when he was the owner of the West Virginia town's Minor League organization, the Charleston Alley Cats. Instead of seeing Kim's achievements as monumental for the sport, he saw the possibility of a publicity stunt.

By early 1992, Kim had temporarily set aside baseball and enrolled in a Broadcast Journalism and Communications degree program at Northwestern University. Throughout her schooling, she continued to keep in touch with Major League scout Don Golan. She had hired him as her agent shortly after the tryout camp in Iowa. Don, after thirty years in the business of coaching and scouting, had been eyeing the opportunity to try something new. He had watched countless numbers of young male athletes pass through his teams and camps, yet none of those men held half the potential that he saw in Kim Reedeaux. Don knew Kim was going to be a star and he was proud to be in her corner.

In June of 1992, the Cubs traded for a prominent young right fielder from their cross-town rivals, the White Sox. Charlie Dirges, moved by the hope that the Cubs' faithful fans would support the trade and quench the complaints about the way he handled the team, also hoped the new player would give the team more power in the line-up. This young star, in his third Major League season, was set to bat third and with what Dirges felt to be a strong lead-off man, Charlie believed his motive for the trade would pay in large dividends; but when the All-Star Break approached and the Cubs had dropped nine of their last twelve games, it became clear that he needed a ploy. The season appeared to be a lost cause, so Charlie decided that the record did not matter, yet the revenue did. Shortly thereafter, Don Golan's phone rang.

"Donny…" Charlie began, "I need a favor."

"You cannot have my girl, Charlie," Don told him bluntly.

"How'd you know I was going to ask?" Charlie inquired.

"C'mon, Charlie; think about it. Losing season, fans are angered, and you need an edge."

"I need a ballplayer." Charlie said.

"You need a publicity stunt and you're not using Kim," Don said as he hung up the phone.

Two days passed and Charlie was still intrigued by Kim's skill level. She had joined the Chicago City League's baseball program as a youth instructor and her ability to break down the game to a level that young children could understand was unlike anything he had ever seen. Kim was an all-around talent. That was as clear as the blue sky above the haven at Addison and Sheffield on any given day. It showed in her play; it showed in her life; it showed in her style; and it showed in her heart. To Kim, the game was not about salaries or contracts, endorsements or advertising. The game was about the smell of the grass, the sounds of the cheers, the skies of blue, and the excitement that came from nine players, win or lose, standing as one by the end of the day, knowing they had put forth their best effort. That was the definition of baseball for Kim Reedeaux.

Charlie, after seeing Kim's demeanor with the boys during the City League outing, knew he had to bring Kim onto his Major League roster and he set forth to change Don Golan's mind.

"Donny…" Charlie said, as he again spoke with Golan.

"I'm not doing it, Charlie," Don said.

"Donny…listen…" Charlie said, sternly. "I know you want what is best for Kim and I know you think I have bad intentions…"

"Yes," Golan agreed.

"…but, I saw Kim with those City League boys and she is fabulous."

"What about the law, Charlie? Huh? How are you planning to get around the law?" Don reminded him.

"What law?" Charlie asked.

"The 1952 law banning women from Major League play," Don stated.

"I'll work out something. I'll call the Commissioner; I'll take care of it."

"I bet you will," Don said, unconvincingly.

"If, through the Commissioner's Office, I am able to make an exception, just for Kim, will you allow me to sign her?"

"She has no Minor League experience, Charlie; she isn't ready for this," Don argued.

"Okay, what if I put her in the system at Double A–West Tennessee? We'll let her pitch a few games there, and then we'll advance her to the Majors, just to see if she's ready; would that be acceptable?" Charlie asked.

"If you can pull it off, I'll agree," Don announced. "But I do not think you will ever pull it off."

"Give me until Monday," Charlie said, confidently, as he disconnected.

Charlie had given himself a deadline to complete what he believed, deep in his heart, to be the impossible task of convincing the Commissioner of Major League Baseball to overturn a ruling that had been the benchmark of America's Pastime since 1952, for one player and one player alone. More than that, he had given himself only seven days to complete the task.

As Charlie reached for his newspaper, he noticed the title to a sports column that read in the trademark style of Merv Griffin's hit game show, Jeopardy: "A Cubs' World Series. What is 'Something That Only a Miracle Can Provide'?" Once he read the headlines, Charlie knew that a call to the MLB Commissioner's Office in New York City was a must.

The date was Tuesday, July 21, 1992, and though, at the time, it seemed like another hot summer day, the significance of the phone call the Cubs' General Manager made eventually altered the history of baseball forever. At 7:30 that morning and a good hour and a half before he usually arrived, Charlie Dirges arrived at his front office suite with one goal in mind: the creation of a ploy so solidly founded and so convincing that Baseball's Commissioner would have to permit it. The Cubs' organization – but mainly Charlie – was willing to stop at nothing. Charlie wanted Kim. If lying is what it took to make that happen, he was willing to spend hours in confession for his actions at a later date in time. On that day, the Church of Baseball was his top priority; he knew the Lord would forgive the rest. He knew God must be a Cubs fan given how tested and supportive their beloved fans are.

That day was a bright and sunny day in Chicago and the Cubs had managed a 2–3 record since returning from the mid-season All-Star Break. With the team in the middle of a ten-game road trip, Charlie phoned the Commissioner regarding Kim. The team's record, at that time, was 42–50, eight games under .500.

The Honorable Richard W. Duffy, Junior, was Major League Baseball's Commissioner in 1992 and it was a position that he had proudly held through scandal and sorrow. Known for being fair, but firm, in his decision-making, Duffy's aura was a quality taken differently and not overly appreciated by the sport's owners and general managers throughout his tenure. Duffy assisted when arbitration issues arose, but had never ruled on such a game-changing aspect as allowing a woman to play at the Major League level. Charlie Dirges was unmoved by the past; he wanted to give his ball club something that would prove his focus on the future: a glimmer of hope, or maybe a good laugh, if his ploy succeeded and Kim proved to be a joke.

The phone conversation between Commissioner Duffy and General Manager Dirges was long and at times, heated. By the time that the two said their good-byes, it seemed as though there was a better likelihood of Dirges' resignation from the Cubs' organization than permitting a woman in the game. Still, Charlie had set his deadline with Kim's agent and he knew that time was of the essence. He needed a back-up plan, just in case.

After he came to the conclusion that nothing was going to come from the phone call, Charlie Dirges headed to O'Hare Airport and chartered a plane to meet with Commissioner Duffy, face-to-face in New York.

Dirges and Duffy conferred over a dinner of chicken tikka masala at the Haveli Restaurant, where both men weighed the pros and cons of the situation. If Kim played, even in Minor League ball, the floodgates would open for the integration of women throughout the league. That was something both Dirges and Duffy saw as a blessing or a curse.

The move to allow Kim's Major League participation would more than likely sharply increase interest in the sport by women, helping drive more fans, revenue, and advertising opportunities. Yet, there were many statistics to show that baseball was already quite popular among women in its current form, seemingly quashing that theory. Of course, there was also the problem of having male athletes who were content to keep the sport as it was. Would the seasoned veterans who had done something one way for close to two decades suddenly understand the changes that bringing a woman into the league would require? Maybe yes, maybe no. By bringing a female into the game, the worry of harassment and in some cases, dissension by the male athletes who were adamantly against the change was a concern. Many times, as women tried to survive in male-dominated sports before, they did so quite successfully. What good and what message would Kim's possible failure send to young women? The decision mandated much consideration. Such a historic decision could never happen instantaneously. Charlie Dirges knew that if, by Monday, some progress occurred, Don Golan would cut him some slack. That was the kind of man that Don was. He was all for progress but realized that progress did not happen overnight.

When the dinner meeting was finished, Commissioner Duffy shook Dirges' hand and agreed to strongly consider his position. The Commissioner clearly understood the pitfalls of easing the long-withstanding sanctions against women playing the game professionally, but he also saw the long-term potential that such a move would bring. At that point in time, baseball had left fans with nothing to become excited or inflamed about since Hank Aaron's all-time home run record in 1974 or Roger Maris' 61st home run in 1961. Both records were shrouded in some controversy. Certainly, the admission of women ballplayers in the Majors would stir the cauldron of discord with some supporters too. Yet, after long consideration, it was a move that Commissioner Duffy agreed upon, for a trial basis anyway.

At 4:15 p.m. on Monday, July 27, 1992, Charlie Dirges' phone rang. With forty-five minutes to go before his deadline with Don Golan passed, Commissioner Duffy was on the line.

"I have ruled on your request, Charlie," Duffy announced.

"And…" Charlie said, his knees quivering nervously.

"I have agreed to allow your girl to play in the Minor Leagues. If she proves herself in Single A–ball, she will have the opportunity to advance to Double A–West Tennessee. If she proves herself there, she can come to Iowa, and if Ms. Reedeaux serves to show all of us that she is as talented as you claim, I will issue a sanction that allows her to play in the Majors. But she will have to prove herself. No special circumstances and no special privileges. She will board the team bus on travel days, practice just like her male counterparts, and play by the current Minor League regulations. Unsuccessful following of these mandates, letter by letter, will lead to her departure. Understood?"

"Yes, sir," Charlie said. "I will call Golan." Dirges thought that calling Golan would be one of the most enjoyable phone calls he had ever made. He soon realized how wrong he was.

"Hi, Donny," Charlie began. "I did it; I got Kim into Single A–ball."

"We did not agree on Single A–ball, did we?" Don reminded him.

"Yes, I know. You said Double A–West Tennessee."

"I stand by that," Don stated firmly.

Dirges bickered with Golan on the phone and in person for nearly another week about whether Kim would play in Single A–ball. During that time, the outlook on Cubs' season had begun to improve. From July 21st through July 28th, the Cubs had managed six wins and only one loss, including a sweep of the Cincinnati Reds. The team appeared to be on an upward swing. The Cubs were three games under .500; the players' morale began to improve, and it looked like the "gimmick," as some had called Kim's potential baseball debut, was no longer needed. That is why Don Golan, Kim's agent, finally decided to let her become a member of the Cubs' Single A affiliate in Peoria, Illinois.

Kim left her home in Chicago on August 1, 1992, to begin her career as a semi-professional baseball player. As she rode the train from Chicago to Peoria, Kim closed her eyes and thought of the women from baseball's past who paved the way for this day to come. Jackie Mitchell, the first woman to sign a Minor League contract, most inspired Kim that day. Women had played a role in the game of baseball for a century, yet their impact on the sport had been limited. Kim Reedeaux hoped to change the viewpoint.

Twenty-plus years later, it was safe to say that her efforts had garnered support. As she sat in the Cubs' home dugout and watched the deep purple storm clouds pass swiftly overhead, she heard a fan cry, "Rain, rain, go away, Kim deserves a chance to play!" The chant was soon echoed throughout all of Cub Nation in attendance for that life-or-death Game 7. A carnival-like atmosphere was soon born from such a silly rhyming phrase. Besides drier weather conditions, on that late October night, the fans knew what they wanted. They wanted Kim to cream one over the center field wall. Yet, as the rain continued, Kim just sat in the dugout and smiled. She admired the support she had received from the faithful fans on Chicago's North Side. Yet, everything she had ever known and everything she felt that night changed in an instant when her manager notified her that a phone call awaited. It was the biggest night of her life, Game 7 of the World Series, and Kim was in a situation that appeared to be life-or-death for her team's season. During that World Series Game 7 rain delay, however, Kim learned that there are more important things than baseball. It was then that she received word from her mother that her father had suffered a heart attack.

CHAPTER 14

Some of the biggest dilemmas in life come suddenly. When an unforeseen health mishap arises and needs immediate attention, the dilemma always seems to surface when we are least prepared for it. That was exactly what was happening for Kim Reedeaux. Kim had spent the entire evening under the impression that her parents were in the stands, watching her every move. In reality, they had never been at the game. Instead, they were five miles from Wrigley in the Critical Care Unit of the Regional Medical Center and had seen nothing more than EKG print-outs and CAT scan results.

Under normal circumstances, Kim felt she should notify her manager, leave the stadium, and join her family at the hospital. That is what any daughter would want – the opportunity to be there for her family – and especially her father – in their time of greatest need. But, this was the World Series, the last game of a long season and the Cubs' last chance to end their Championship drought. As she sat on the hard pinewood dugout bench, contemplating her next move, Kim thought back to her first Major League at-bat and the decisions that went along with it.

Just as the Cubs' General Manager had predicted, Kim had quickly graduated from Single A–ball to the team's Double A–West Tennessee Farm Club. By May 1993, Kim was a twenty-year-old powerhouse. At shortstop, she could knock down a long fly ball with her bare hands and turn double plays on a dime. From the pitcher's mound, she could hurl a 97-mph fastball with such ease that her delivery was nearly an art form, one that many of her teammates, all male of course, had given the name, "Kim's Gem." Each player wanted to perfect her style.

In A-ball, Kim had experienced no animosity from the men on her team. They were all gifted ballplayers whose outlook and goals were the same – get to the Majors, as soon as possible and in the most effective way. Double A–ball at West Tennessee had proven to be much different, especially when she met Rick Chapman, the eighteen-year-old cousin of Cubs' pitcher Leon Chapman. Yes, that Leon Chapman – the man who was beneath signing a young girl's baseball, the superstar who was against the participation of women in the sport, the egotist, the bigot, and to some, the baby.

Rick Chapman had been an All-Star since his Little League days. His team had won the Little League World Series in fine fashion and had been in the running for greatness more times than one could mention. Rick, like his cousin, had timeless issues with women's involvement in athletics and especially, in baseball. "It is a stag sport." That was Rick's motto. Rick, for one, cringed when little Melissa Mackenzie was invited to join his Little League team, this side of a decade ago. In every instant and fashion that arose when Melissa's play was less than 300%, Rick rebuked her. One hundred percent was not good enough for a woman in the sport. I do not think 1,000% would have been enough either. A woman could give 10,000% effort and in Rick's mind, that would not be enough. Rick's philosophy, much like his cousin's, was treat women like crap and they will let go of their silly baseball fantasies. Babies, barbecues, and putting up with ball jokes are all that women are good for – right? In his mind, yes.

The Cubs selected Rick Chapman in the June 1992 draft. He quickly advanced from A-ball in Daytona to Double A at West Tennessee. Many scouts believed he would receive his call to the Big Leagues before he could reach Triple A at Iowa. Rick was a solid third baseman, something the Cubs had not seen since the future Hall-of-Famer Ron Santo left the Cubs in 1973. Better still, Rick was a switch-hitter. Regardless of his better qualities, however, one thing remained – he had no regard for women, in baseball or in life. Needless to say, when Kim Reedeaux arrived, Rick was unhappy. He was more than unhappy; he was enraged.

While most of the Double A ball players were as humble and welcoming as her teammates in Daytona had been, Rick Chapman went out of his way to make Kim feel uncomfortable. He was a practical joker by nature and often used that trait to his advantage. Rick also held the idea that women were inferior and gullible, thus worthy of his disrespect. In the star third baseman's mind, those two ideals went hand in hand.

When the moment arose and the appropriate gag came to mind, Rick was determined to initiate Kim to Double A ball in a fashion that she would not soon forget. He took a jar of Jif peanut butter, a jar of grape jelly, and an old turkey baster, and painted the inside of Kim's cleats with the concoction. Then, he plastered the underside of her baseball cap with hot sauce. Rick, however, underestimated Kim's level of intelligence.

She knew he was a joker and that he was against her position, one hundred percent. Rick and his cousin, Leon, could have been human clones. With Rick on the pitcher's mound, Kim prepared her things for practice. Then she walked onto the field with her hair ideally styled and her uniform as pressed and neat as one would expect. Rick was stunned. How could Kim have known? ESP, perhaps, or maybe, WOW – Woman Oriented Wit.

When Rick arrived in the locker room, a note was awaiting him. The note read: "Look at your car; you have to get up earlier!" As Rick rushed to the parking lot, he found his brand new black 1993 Pontiac Trans Am convertible completely covered in hot sauce, peanut butter, and jelly. Rick tried to force Kim to pay for the damage to his vehicle. He took the matter to the management of the West Tennessee team numerous times. The answer from management was the same: "Do not mess with her and she will not mess with you."

Two months had passed before Rick finally gave up fighting for his car's damage. His attitude during those post-prank months had begun to cause problems among members of the team and adversely affected what should have been the main focus – winning baseball games. When the rumors began to circulate about a possible trade that would send him to the Akron Aeros, a Double A affiliate of the Cleveland Indians, Rick decided that there were other ways to manage Kim.

During the Major League All-Star Break, Rick placed a phone call to his cousin, Leon. The younger Chapman offered his condolences for the fact that Leon missed making the All-Star team. Then, enraged, Rick asked his cousin what could be done ensure Kim's failure. At that stage in the year, Kim was placing career numbers in the record books. She was batting nearly .400, had stolen 19 bases, turned 13 double plays from shortstop and as a pitcher, she had thrown a one-hit complete game. In early July, it appeared that Rick's certain call to the Majors, or at least to Triple A–Iowa, was destined to come after Kim's beckoning. That was an idea that Rick was not ready to accept. The "beaten by a girl" stigma was indeed a sticking point.

Leon did not have many suggestions for Rick, in spite of their joint disrespect for Kim's attempts at greatness. He did, however, make Rick a solemn promise. Leon assured Rick that if Kim would reach the

Majors, as a member of the Cubs, he would see to it that she did not last. To those who opposed Kim's persistence, there was only one offense in baseball worse than a female's attempt to thrive in a man's world – witnessing a female who cheated in order to gain an edge.

Kim Reedeaux was an honest person. She was as tough as nails on the outside, yet as pure as winter's first snowfall on the inside. She firmly believed in treating everyone with respect and dignity. Consequently, she also believed in standing up for one's beliefs. If that meant fighting for a cause, she was not against it, and if that meant dishing payback for a wrong, she was willing to do just that, as long as the revenge did not compromise her principles or morals. Kim was never unlawful, nor did she tolerate those who condoned illegal activity. That is why, when Leon Chapman enacted his plan, Kim was not ousted from the League. In the end, baseball management knew better of Kim; the way she conducted herself proved better than that.

The date was September 30, 1993. The Cubs were playing their 162nd game in a season that had seen several high points and other areas that still needed some improvement. The team's season had been more productive than in years past. The Cubs had battled hard for most of the year and found themselves with an 83–78 record going into the final game.

Kim had received the call to Triple A–Iowa three weeks before, and looked forward to what the future held. What she did not know was the moment she had been awaiting since childhood was about to occur.

Kim's Triple A debut was magnificent. With an overabundance of quality pitchers on the roster, Kim had settled for playing shortstop. Her batting average and on-base percentage were both exceptional and it was safe to say that she had turned more than one head in the Cubs' Front Office.

One week before the end of the regular season, the Cubs' General Manager contacted Commissioner Duffy's office to be certain that a ruling allowed Kim Reedeaux the opportunity to play at the Major League level, despite the 1952 law that prohibited her participation. Once the team received confirmation, in writing, that the Commissioner approved a temporary override of the law, the Cubs placed a phone call to Iowa. Kim Reedeaux was set to make her Major League debut.

Her long-awaited first appearance would come during that final game of the 1993 season. The Cubs were on the road, playing their third game in as many days against the San Diego Padres at Jack Murphy Stadium. The Padres were finishing a very forgettable season and had reached the 100-loss mark in losing to the Cubs during the first game of that series. For the most part, Kim's Chicago Cubs' teammates were very enthusiastic about her debut. After all, the club was in fourth place and the season was over; there could be no harm in giving the girl a shot.

Pitching for the Cubs that day was none other than Leon Chapman. Leon had posted career numbers of his own in the 1993 season and looked to be in the running for his second gold glove. He had pitched in thirty-one games and with the help of his teammates, had secured fifteen victories to lead the pitching staff.

Yet, having tallied fifteen wins for a team no better than fourth place in the division, Leon was bitter. He had played in the Majors for five seasons and had yet to call himself a "winner." In Leon's mind, a "winner" meant the effort of every man on the team and to him, a fourth-place finish did not describe the fact that three teams were better, it described that the Cubs were worse.

As a result of his anger, Leon decided to ruin the day and possibly the career of young Kim Reedeaux. He remembered the vow he had made to his cousin that July afternoon during the All-Star Break. A promise to a family member was a promise. When no one was looking, Leon switched the corked bat that Kim had been using in batting practice for her game bat, leaving the corked bat for usage in the game.

Leon knew that Kim was a power-hitter and he knew that Eddie Deekus, the Padres' pitcher, threw nothing but junk. His pitches were slow, his control was inconsistent, at best, and his delivery lacked finesse. Despite questions all season from San Diego media personnel regarding why Deekus was still a Major Leaguer, he was. Why bother sending someone to the minors on the last day of a depressing season? It was too late to turn back the clock; the season was over. The final game was not even enough to save face.

In Leon's mind, it stood to reason that Kim would easily find success at the plate off Eddie's lackluster ability. He knew, though, that when Kim creamed the Padres' pitcher's slow-as-molasses curveball, her bat would break. Once the bat broke, exposing the cork, an investigation would ensue, and her career in the Majors would be over for good. In the eyes of his managers and fellow athletes, Leon was all about what was "best for the team," but to him, Kim was not an athlete, she was a girl and thus a detriment.

When game time arrived, Leon sat and twirled a toothpick for entertainment. Kim was sixth in the batting order when the lineup card was completed. Although it was a road game for the Cubbies, the excitement surrounding Kim's debut had created a stir from the traveling Cub faithful. While only 13,554 fans were in attendance for the game's historical significance, the fans' excitement disrupted play for a minute and a half during the second inning when Kim stepped to the plate for her first Major League at-bat. The fans cheered when patience beat her nerves and Kim drew a walk on four straight pitches. They cheered again when she trotted home to score the first run of the ballgame. Even the fans adorned in the Padres' home colors were proud of Kim's accomplishment. After all, San Diego fans had not witnessed much enthusiasm in their home park the entire season.

The Cubs scored their second run of the ballgame, three pitches later, and in a move that went against the great Leon Chapman's plan, the San Diego manager yanked Eddie Deekus from game, much to the dismay of the home fans in attendance who had been quite entertained by the fallacies of their pitcher. Leon's agenda worsened when San Diego Manager David Pelcher called for Eric Chavez, a right-handed, long reliever who had been a starter in the Cardinals organization earlier in his career.

Although he was thirty-five years of age, Chavez had the mound presence of a young athlete just entering his prime. Leon knew that it would be next to impossible for Kim to hit the ball. More so, he realized she was not likely to shatter her bat by crushing one of Chavez's pitches. To the baseball aficionado, the box score for Leon's grand scheme looked bleak. No baseball game – or scheme – is finished until the last out is recorded.

From his entrance in the game's second inning through the match-up's eighth frame, Eric Chavez was nearly perfect. He had walked just one batter, while fanning seven more. Luck had left the Padres before the season. Tommy Tynan, Padres' middle reliever and superstar who had tallied career numbers of his own during the 1993 campaign, still poured his heart and soul into every pitch. For the Padres, the season was, by all accounts, finished. The Cubs had maintained their 2–1 lead for seven innings and it was obvious that the game was not a save situation.

If you were managing the Padres on the last day of the season, what would you have done? Would you have left your star pitcher in the game, giving him one last shot of adrenaline-driven glory in an easily forgotten season, or, would you have removed him from the game to replace his skills for those of one, Tommy Tynan? If you said, "Leave in the pitcher who brought you this far," you would have been wrong. The Padres' skipper came to the mound and motioned for right-handed reliever Tommy Tynan.

Tynan entered the game with a difficult task. He was set to face the heart of the Cubs' batting order and if one runner reached base, Kim Reedeaux would again be at the plate. The first batter in the Cubs' ninth inning was Darby Daniels, the North Siders' talented first baseman. On a 2–2 count, Darby launched a rocket that bounced off the center field wall for a stand-up double. Worse than that for the Padres, the lead-off double assured that Kim Reedeaux would have one more at-bat. The next two Cubs batters walked on four straight pitches to load the bases with Kim Reedeaux poised at the plate. The bases loaded situation gave Kim the potential to break the game wide-open for an almost certain season-ending Cubs victory.

After three warm-up swings, Kim stood attentively at the plate; she was ready for whatever pitch combination that Tommy Tynan and Padres' catcher Dennis Shallot had chosen. The first throw was a 98-mph fastball that just clipped the corner of the plate for strike one. The second was a 96-mph slider that the home plate umpire called a ball. Tynan's third pitch was waist high and centered down the middle of the plate. Kim knew what she had to do and she gave it her all. She connected with the ball with such upper arm strength that the pitch carried on the breeze and landed on the other side of the center field wall. The ball, hit with such force and magnitude, sailed so quickly that it needed a nifty quip from NASA personnel. The fans were in such awe that many did not notice Kim's shattered bat. The drama on the field meant little to the fan, still trying to determine what they had just witnessed. Soon, the umpiring crew chief summoned the rest of his staff to home plate to examine the lumber. The umpires determined quickly that the bat violated standards of play. In the Majors, modifying a baseball bat in any way leads to the violation of Rule 6.06 (d), which loosely states that a batter is subject to ejection and suspension if found with a corked bat and in the event of such an offense, no advancement on the bases shall be permitted. Also, the player found to have committed said offense is subject to additional fines as determined by the League and/or the individual team. From 1970 through that final game of the 1993 season, Kim's corked bat was only the third such item to violate Major League rules.

From a distance, Leon Chapman knew that his effort to botch Kim's debut had proven to be successful. As Kim's teammates and the fans at Jack Murphy Stadium sat quietly, rather stunned by what was taking place, Leon sat alone, basking in silent joy for what he viewed as a "job well done."

Kim was immediately ejected from the game and told she would have to face the Cubs' President the following Monday. Throughout the process, Kim continued to voice her innocence. Still, the sportswriters, media outlets, and fans were all hesitant to believe her. The gist of each discussion centered on permanently banning Kim from the sport. After all, the 1952 ban of women in baseball remained in place for all other women; Kim was merely an exception. The general consensus was "If she cannot play fairly, and must cheat to gain an edge, she shouldn't play." The idea would have been a plausible statement had Kim purposefully used a botched bat, but she and her truest followers knew that she had done nothing wrong. Soon, a videotape surfaced to prove her innocence was true.

A major cable movie network had been filming a documentary about Kim's debut during that final game at Jack Murphy Stadium. The film crew had spent countless hours tailing Kim through the Triple A baseball schedule and recorded that final day of the season from both the field and the team's locker room. Doug Elkhorn, the docu-drama's narrator, had been on the field when Leon Chapman placed a dark, wooden bat in the bat rack. That bat had looked identical to the one Kim had used: the corked bat used in game play. Upon Major League Baseball's review of the videotape from the documentary shoot, it was determined that Kim had not botched her own bat.

Although she was not entirely guilty for the corked bat incident, Kim still agreed to pay a fine to Major League Baseball and issue a public statement to the sport and team's fans; she also agreed that, in the event she would return for a full season in 1994, she would accept a three-game suspension. Kim, the modest and grateful woman she had become, was willing to accept some form of punishment. Despite the fact she did not botch her bat, she had used it in the game; the fact she had upset her. The question was: Did she really want to come back again?

Kim had proven that she could reach the Majors; she had beaten all the odds stacked against her to have one moment certain to live within her memory forever. She had made countless friends, several enemies, and had shown the world that one person's voice and willpower had the potential to make a difference. Yet, even as strongly as she knew that to be true, Kim also had to face the fact that in spite of her efforts to clear her name, she would always be associated with the end-of-the-season corked bat incident. She worried that one corked bat would forever overshadow her future accomplishments; just as Pete Rose's betting scandal still overshadows his on-the-field success. She feared the impact the incident would have on her team. More than that, she was apprehensive about how her own self-esteem would carry, as she moved forward from that occurrence.

As the winter approached, Kim was set to make the hardest decision of her life. She pondered the dilemma over Christmas, realizing that Spring Training was two and a half months away. After much thought, Kim decided that, if invited, she would be there.

When Spring Training for the 1994 season arrived, Kim blessed the coaches and fans in Arizona with a terrible March campaign. She misplayed long fly balls and overthrew pitches that should have led to double plays. At the plate, she had gone 2-for-19. Even as poorly as she had played, Kim was still the last person cut from the roster. After packing her things and saying goodbye to her teammates, Kim headed back to the Cubs' Triple A affiliate in Iowa, with nary a bitter bone in her body.

Kim knew her effort during the season preview was subpar. She told a sportswriter that she wanted to demote herself to the Minors. Sure enough, her bid to make the Big Leagues in 1994 failed. She was understandably disappointed but vowed to fight much harder to improve herself. Kim had been a fighter since her first day of life and nothing would ever come along to change that. After all, despite her poor spring outing, Kim's off-season decision to remain a baseball player was a choice she had made on her own.

Now, with her father hospitalized after a heart attack and the rain beginning to slacken at Wrigley Field, Kim was once again faced with a difficult decision: to be with her family or to wait out the rain. Once more, she felt she was able to reach a compromise. Only, this time, Kim's decision proved to bring no regrets.

CHAPTER 15

There is an old saying passed from generation to generation, "If at first you don't succeed, try, and try again." When a baseball player finds success in the Majors, then returns to the Minor Leagues, there is a certain amount of despondence, interspersed with a sense of hope. Nearly every ballplayer to have ever found success in the Majors will attest to the fact that nothing comes easily and, pardon all pun-like references, good things do come to those who are willing to wait for them.

Kim Reedeaux had paid just one year of dues in Minor League Baseball when she received her call to mingle with the big league crowd. Some people would (and did) call her gifted and fortunate, aside from the infamous corked bat incident. Others simply believed her to be a one-trick pony of sorts who had her chance and irreparably "blew it." Critics, however, are in all facets of life. Kim knew that and henceforth, did not allow the criticism to stand in the way of her dream. She had seen the style of Major League Baseball and in just one game she had learned lessons that would last her a lifetime, whether she was a participant in the sport or a spectator.

As the 1994 Iowa Cubs' season began, Kim was the star of the show, not for her ability at the plate but for that one game where, whether credited or not, she took a big league pitcher to the depths of infinity, crushing the ball from the ballpark. Her experience during the last game of the Major League regular season was the goal of every Single, Double or Triple A participant, the hope of every high school player, and the dream of every Little Leaguer, despite their location. Her opportunity was something that young children only saw in their sleep and the reason behind their unrelenting passion for the game.

In the five months since Kim's Major League debut, she had received over two tons of mail. Each card or letter brought with it some semblance of congratulations or some sentiment that praised or placed her alongside the iconic heroes of the era. She had heard from grandmothers, pre-schoolers, Little League coaches and retired Major Leaguers. She took the time to read each and every note herself. She had received requests for interviews from the most highly regarded media personnel and the smallest of media markets.

Critics aside, the majority of America's baseball fans fully supported the Cubs' choice to bring Kim to the Majors. The largest nationally distributed newspaper even went so far as to conduct a survey, polling the country's opinion of Kim Reedeaux, the shortstop. As a whole, at least on paper, the citizens of these United States appeared to have supported Kim Reedeaux's Major League debut, more so than they supported the President's Middle East policies. Kim Reedeaux had become a marketing tool, whether she had wanted to become one or not. And, I can tell you from personal knowledge, she did not wish that position for the world.

Kim Reedeaux was a dreamer and someone who wanted the most from life, as she saw it. She was not someone who lived by how everyone else expected her life to be. She had chosen the goal she had hoped to fulfill and at age twenty-two, she believed she had done a brilliant job. Still, Kim was obstinate and appreciated not only her freedom, but also her privacy. The country's most popular columnists had stated early in Kim's quest for Major League immortality that her private and stubborn side would eventually be her downfall.

Kim, however, had one thing in her favor. The ability to be as tough-as-nails when warranted, yet as sweet as could be when needed. She had a knack for being polite, yet firm, when faced with criticism, and many times she had been known for putting columnists in their places with such finesse that the interviewer believed he was receiving a compliment. Harold Reedeaux had often spoken of his daughter's multi-faceted lifestyle as that of a Rubik's cube: "Always colorful, yet hard to line up." His analogy was dead-to-rights.

Whether the day was sunny and hot or dreary and cold, Kim Reedeaux was constantly laughing and always smiling. Her style made her the hero of many baseball fans and the enemy of many baseball analysts. In spite of it all, Kim preferred her ties to the former, moreover than the latter. Kim spent most of her childhood in Pittsburgh. Yet she incorporated her parents' small town upbringing and simple-minded beliefs into her life every day. She was not pursuing her Major League goals for the sake of the media; she was not seeking to make a statement, even if such a feat was inevitable. Kim Reedeaux was a baseball player because she wanted to be. Her choice was not based upon wealth or fame, nor was she pushed into baseball by parents who used their children to glorify themselves – neither route can bring a person true happiness. Kim based her decision to pursue her career and happily remain in baseball's Minor League level solely on her admiration and respect for the game – plain and simple.

By the middle of May, the media frenzy had invaded Kim's livelihood like a swarm of bees on a honeycomb. She could not walk without pushing away a microphone; she could not eat without hearing her name on a newscast; she could not sleep due to late night phone calls from beat reporters who hoped she would be at their beck and call. The passion that the media acquired for the young powerhouse was beginning to take its toll on the Iowa Triple-A club. The team had begun the season with a five-game winning streak. By the end of April, the team was three games over .500, but on May 1, 1994, a prominent sports magazine in the Midwest area, *America's Pastime Report*, broke the rumor that Kim Reedeaux was about to be called to the Big Leagues again, which refueled the controversial fire. Should she return? Should she still serve her suspension, though not guilty of the corking incident? Should she pitch or play the middle infield? The storylines were never ending and each one began from a highly unfounded piece of inner-city gossip.

With increased pressure mounting on the team, Kim chose to enact one of the most admirable choices that a baseball player could make. She chose to step aside from the sport she so loved for the betterment of her team. Or, at least, that is what she had hoped to do. Kim's decision to quit the team had been an easy one; convincing her supporters, coaches, and teammates that she actually believed in her decision proved to be a difficult formality. On the pretense of hosting a press conference to "clear the air" about the previous season's antics, once and for all, Kim sat with her agent, coach, and family in the conference room of Chicago's Radisson Hotel.

"For the sake of the team," Kim began. "I have decided to step aside from baseball, return to Northwestern University and continue to pursue my degree in Broadcast Journalism and Communications." A hail of boos from the crowd interrupted her speech. "I know what you are thinking," she continued. "You are thinking the pressure finally got to me; you would be wrong." The echo of more boos ensued, as if the crowd did not believe her. "I have loved each moment of my baseball playing career, but I know that my team, my coaches, and everyone associated with Chicago Cubs baseball, on all levels, would be better off, if the pressure I have placed upon them was removed." Kim took no questions from reporters and fought back tears as she walked from the stage to the echoing of her name from those in attendance. Shortly thereafter, she returned to Iowa, packed her locker, and traveled back to her Chicago apartment, confident that she had given up baseball for good.

While Kim had planned on returning to civilian life, her arrival back in Chicago proved that her intent would be harder than she had expected. Kim began to realize the magnitude of the iconic following she had amassed, thanks in part to one baseball game and one wrongful scandal. Everywhere she went, someone knew her. Windows of small businesses and t-shirts of young baseball fans who strolled with their Irish setters along the banks of Lake Michigan plastered her picture. Harry Caray's Restaurant, where Kim had first mapped the plan for her baseball career, had a corner shrine of newspaper clippings about the league's female phenom. Simply stated, Kim had stepped aside from the game of baseball, but the mounted pressure had not eased from her.

Accordingly, Kim felt the need to remove herself completely from the gossip and pressure that had mounted in her life. The next week, she flew to South Bend, Indiana and interviewed with the administration at the University of Notre Dame, and for the sake of privacy, she adopted her mother's maiden name for the duration of her collegiate career. It was there that Kim came to meet Craig Credan, someone who became somewhat memorable for his Wrigley Field seat position, a little over nine years later.

Craig Credan was an engineering student when Kim Crossdale (Reedeaux) briefly crossed paths with him in 1994. He was a quiet young man who led a carefree and peaceful young life until the night of October 14, 2003. Credan had been the consummate Cub fan; over the course of his entire life and like Cub fans worldwide he had suffered the agony of team's defeat and endured countless years of the Cubs' curse-ridden bad luck.

Conversely, Credan never imagined how the events of one baseball game would change his life forever. On that cool autumn night, Game 6 of the 2003 National League Championship Series (NLCS) took place at Wrigley Field. The Cubs were hosting the Florida Marlins; the winner of that series would play in the World Series. For the Marlins, the 2003 World Series would be their franchise's second Series appearance in only their ninth year as a franchise. For the Cubs, winning the NLCS and reaching the World Series would mean the end of a fifty-nine-year

World Series drought and a chance to end the even longer, ninety-five-year Championship dry spell. The scale tipped in the Cubs' favor. The Cubs had home-field advantage, nestled safely within the walls of the Friendly Confines and surrounded by the support of their hometown fans. The atmosphere at Wrigley Field was nothing short of electric. The Cubs were back at home for Game 6, clinging to a 3–2 lead in the best-of-seven Championship Series. The odds were in the Cubbies' favor. All they had to do was win one of the next two games and the team would be World Series bound for the first time since 1945. Better still, the Cubs had pegged their two best pitchers for duty in games six and seven, should a seventh game be necessary. To the optimistic Cub contingent, the possibility of finally putting to rest all the timeless rumors of curses appeared to be within an arm's length. Yet, an arm's length would, in the minds of many baseball gurus the world over, soon be the team's demise.

Through seven innings, Game 6 of the 2003 NLCS had looked as though the fans of Wrigleyville – the long suffering, yet ever loyal followers of the oft forgotten baseball team on Chicago's North Side – were finally in line for their trip to the Fall Classic. After the seventh frame, the Cubs were leading the Marlins 3–0. But, as the old baseball saying goes, "It ain't over till the final out is tallied."

The Cubs' star pitcher had hurled a gem and had shown little signs of fatigue. With only two innings remaining, his job was clear; his team was six outs away from destiny and he needed to get it done. Whether the pressure of the situation played a factor, no one knows. But, one thing would soon be certain – the Cubs were definitely unlucky.

The story of the eighth inning, that cold October night, would be broadcast and re-broadcast, time and again, on every major sports network. Yes, we all know what happened. The Cubs' left fielder misplayed a ball that he should have recovered and Steve Bartman, the Cub fan in the wrong place and the wrong time, forever staked his own claim in history when he became the sport's most memorable scapegoat. Craig Credan had seen it all.

The scene of the crime, as many Cub fans felt about the event, now known only as the "Bartman Incident," was aisle 4; row 8; seat 113, one row behind Craig Credan's position in the stands that night. Over the course of Craig's twenty-eight-year life, he had made a yearly pilgrimage to Wrigley Field. He did so for the love of the game and support of what had become his team. He always arrived at the ballpark early and spoke with the ivy and the other heritage-laden factions of

Wrigley Field just like they were long, lost friends with whom he had recently reconnected. He was not crazy by speaking to the ivy. To Craig, talking to the ivy was no worse than talking to his neighbor's dog. The ivy held secrets and history; Craig believed another piece of Wrigley history was destined that night. It was, but not in the manner Craig expected.

Craig's father, Douglas, a career welder, had purchased a baseball glove for his son when Craig was a little more than six months old. Craig's mother, Deanna, believed the purchase was rushed but never said a word. As Craig grew, so did his love for the Cubs and his yearning to see them live. The Credan family began their yearly train trip to Wrigley when Craig was seven and from then onward, Craig had always gone to the game with his glove. That is, he went to every game with his glove, except October 14, 2003.

Who knows what would have happened that night had Craig been at the game with glove in hand. Maybe the suggested interference would not have occurred. Maybe the left fielder would have caught the ball. Still, while Steve Bartman's effort for a souvenir will go down in history as one of baseball's most memorable moments, Craig Credan's face will be just as prominent, shown in every video replay aired, as the individual sports fan ponders "what might have been."

What might have been on that momentous October night was not even a thought to Kim or Craig when they met in 1994. What mattered then was a mutual respect for the Chicago Cubs baseball team and the common interests shared by two college kids. As Kim and Craig progressed in their educational pursuits, their friendship grew and would eventually lead them both back to Wrigley for one night, one game, and one chance to change personal and sports history.

Craig Credan, years later when asked about the Bartman Incident of 2003, still held the belief that everything happens for a reason. Kim knew there was a logical reason why she was a member of the current Chicago franchise. She had paid her dues, earned every bump, and overcome every obstacle thrown in her direction. Therefore, the situation at hand, Game 7 of the World Series, the bottom of the ninth inning, with two runners on base and two retired, and her long-time nemesis, Boston pitcher, Leon Chapman, on the mound, was her time. All she had to do was seize it.

The thought of her friendship with Craig made Kim more determined to excel once World Series play resumed. Craig's outlook had served to inspire Kim's progress, progress that eventually led to her return to the sport. As the rain slowed to mere droplets, Kim passed the time taking practice swings and running in place. She was not a spiteful person or someone who thrived on revenge, even if a little revenge is sometimes necessary. Still, everything within her soul felt as though she owed Leon Chapman some payback. She felt the need for payback against Leon's snubbing her autograph request; she yearned to avenge Leon's bashing of women, words that had made their lives and finding support for women in baseball very difficult; but most of all, she hoped that pay-off would come in the form of assisting her team in their effort to conquer a championship drought, now over a century old.

As Kim remembered her pathway to the Majors, Eric Henley came over the Wrigley Field Public Address System, with the words a capacity crowd and Kim Reedeaux had longed to hear – "Ladies and gentlemen, play will resume in forty-five minutes." While the news brought cheers from the rain-soaked fans at the stadium, the announcement left Kim feeling rather uneasy. She was skilled, she was knowledgeable, and she had been playing the game for longer than many of her younger fans had been alive, but something seemed to be missing. Soon enough, however, that uneasy feeling was vanished. Kim appeared lost in a daze in the moment that little Dustin Daniels, bat boy for the team, handed her the note he had received from a fan. When she opened the folded steno notebook leaflet, she read the words that forever changed her life.

"Hey sis, it's me, Brian." Brian Reedeaux, Kim's long-lost big brother whom she had not seen in nearly twenty-five years, was there and he had come back for the sole purpose of supporting her, just as he had done when she was little. Kim sprang from the bench and ran onto the field. She jumped up and down and waved her arms, but Brian was nowhere. Had it been a dream? Was the note written as another ploy by her nemesis, Leon Chapman? Kim admitted sabotage was possible; Leon had sabotaged her before. Praying for truth and her brother's attendance, Kim planned on going out there and giving her final at-bat of the season every ounce of momentum she could give it, all for the hope her brother was, indeed, there watching her.

The next half hour passed at a snail's pace and as Kim heard the latest update from the Cubs' Public Address announcer, she reflected upon her years in the Cubs' radio booth. "Those were the days," she said to herself. "Those truly were the days!"

CHAPTER 16

For the ultimate dreamer, two things are obvious. Some dreams happen, while others fade away. For the dreams that fade into the darkness of our minds, the outcome is clear that those dreams have not found their time or space, if they're ever meant to be at all. For the rest, the individual paths to reach and live our dreams are as different and unique as the individuals that strive for them. The trails we take to pursue a dream can often twist and turn, like the dirt roads of rural America, throwing individuals in directions directly opposite of the places they wished to be.

Kim Reedeaux's journey back to Major League Baseball had taken many different paths from her one and only game at the Big League level. She had been to Arizona, as a part of the Winter Baseball Program. She had spent four years in South Bend, Indiana, obtaining a broadcast journalism degree. After college, she accepted a position with Cincinnati, Ohio's famed sports talk radio station, WLW-AM, and in early 2002, at the age of twenty-nine, Kim Reedeaux had moved back home to Pittsburgh where she spent one year sharing the airwaves with her father, prior to his retirement from KDKA.

When Harold Reedeaux retired, he handed the reins of his radio program to his daughter and over the course of the next year, she became one of the top female sportscasters in the Midwest. Some people said that she had inherited her father's style, while others believed that she was the exact opposite of her mentor. Regardless, Kim was popular. Her morning drive radio program on KDKA had the highest rating of any sports show in a five-state radius and for her thirtieth birthday, Kim won a coveted award for excellence in sports coverage.

To the outsider, everything in Kim's life appeared to have fallen into place. She had a wonderful career as a sports commentator, a huge following that, in the realm of female sportscasters, only a select few had ever enjoyed, and she had twice turned down offers to spring onto the national scene as a reporter for a highly-regarded cable television network. At that time, Kim had no interest in pursuing a television sports career and to those closest to her, she did not have much interest in remaining on the radio, either. Kim's dream was to get back into Major League Baseball, as a player. Though she knew her increasing age appeared to be narrowing the gap for her dream to ever again be possible, Kim was undeterred. She had planned nearly everything she had accomplished, prior to setting baseball aside for her collegiate career; she had the willpower to start from scratch, if need be, to prove herself, once more.

Fate, by definition, dictates that some occurrences in life are beyond any realm of control. Kim knew that she had talent when it came to hitting, throwing, and catching a baseball. She also knew that her "destiny" bowed its head to whatever the "gurus of the game" believed. The first call she made in her quest to return was to an old friend, Cubs' talent scout Don Golan.

Don did not have a great deal of advice to give Kim that she did not already know. Kim had already figured that she would have to start at the bottom, having been away from the game for going on ten years. Yet, despite her layoff, Golan still believed in his protégé and advised Kim to attend the Cubs' Tryout Camp in Pittsburgh, that June. Kim had agreed to consider it and by mid-May, she appeared in top form and ready for the camp. With the tryout camp three weeks away, Kim felt like the player given a second chance to achieve greatness, though her anxiety kept saying "your time has passed."

Kim arrived to the tryout camp at 7:30 that June morning, two hours before she was needed. By mid-morning, the event Kim had long looked forward to attending seemed overrun by dread and agony as she sat in the oppressive June heat and waited for her "turn to make a fool of herself." Kim had always believed that everything had a time and a place; on that day, she wondered why she had attended the tryout. She could have left, and even considered it, but deep within her soul, Kim felt a sense of hope. It was an ever-present sense of hope that had been inside her heart since she first announced her baseball dream to her family, as a child. Kim knew, as she awaited her tryout, that she was at a disadvantage; her mind listened to the critics that she had met over the years. Yet, she also knew that she had overcome many drawbacks in her life. That tryout camp and her performance were simply two more steps in her journey.

Kim's moment to impress the scouts came at 2:30 that muggy June afternoon. Maybe it was nervousness; maybe it was a lack of stamina, but whatever the reason, Kim did not give the performance of her life, something needed for a female trying to conquer a man's sport.

Kim, already discouraged by her attempt, seemed even more dejected when told by the scouts that she should consider more practice or better yet, another line of work. Kim already had another line of work; she was a sportscaster and a very good one, at that. As she sat alone in her living room, with the answering machine cued to field the phone calls from her well-wishers and those offering their condolences, Kim wondered if her radio career was her calling. She knew the game of baseball; that was obvious. Yet, she began to wonder if her knowledge base should thrive in the broadcasting realm, as opposed to the baseball field. The answer to her question was one telephone call away.

Kevin Geoffen became the new general manager of Chicago's WGN-Radio in March of 2005. From day one, Kevin fielded the one question that all sports fans in the Windy City always die to know. Was he a White Sox fan or a Cubs fan? Playing it safe in his new role, Kevin always ignored the question, much to the local sports fans' chagrin, but that was the story of life in Chicago. The question about Kevin's loyalties circulated in sports discussions quite often and yet, not a single fan seemed able to uncover whether the blood of the station's GM ran in shades of black and white, or Cubbie blue. Then, Kevin had what sports fans would view as "a moment of weakness."

Les Williamson had been the radio voice of the Chicago Cubs for nearly thirty years and he had worked alongside former Cub player Rich Goldwin for fifteen seasons. Neither broadcaster was young, but while Les's devotion to the team was solely as a broadcaster, Rich's fondness ran much deeper. Both broadcasters had considered retirement, yet Lenny Walton, the former GM of WGN-Radio, had always coerced them into continuing for one more year. In the middle of a mediocre 2005 Cubs campaign, Les utilized the baseball broadcasts to openly voice his displeasure with the management of the Cubs. "The team is not as poor as in past years," Les would say. "But they have much more potential than what is being shown."

Such an attitude from the broadcast booth had served well for the talk-radio chatter circuit, but did not bode well for Les's continued employment. By early July, Les's on-air criticism and antics had filtered their way to the team level. The team, after hearing and reading of Les's disparagement, began an eight-game losing streak. After all, if the radio play-by-play announcer was not on the side of the ball club, what was the incentive to play well? That was, at least, the thought process of several team members.

As a result of the dissension between the ball club and its radio play-by-play radio announcer, Kevin made an unwelcome decision. He called Les Williamson, the thirty-year broadcast veteran, into his office on the first day of the 2005 All-Star Break and strongly suggested that he take his retirement. The company gave Les two options: resign or retire from the organization that had been his bread and butter for the past three decades. Les knew a third option meant termination, so he chose what was much easier to stomach for a veteran unwilling to quit. Les retired.

With Les's retirement, Kevin needed a strong play-by-play voice for the WGN-Radio broadcasts. On an interim basis, Kevin had hired a sportscaster from the WGN-TV booth to take the helm. The General Manager's problem seemed immense, especially in the middle of the season. Therefore, Kevin planned to utilize his temporary replacement for the rest of the season, hoping to hire some "fresh blood" in the off-season. Kevin's nightmare scenario and search would prove to be short-lived, however. The answer he needed would come in the next series that Wrigley Field and the Chicago Cubs hosted.

Kevin had wanted to find a solid play-by-play analyst who knew the game, whether as a fan with experience in broadcasting or as a former player with insight into the behind-the-scenes aspect of the sport, itself. When the Cubs returned to Wrigley Field, after the All-Star Break to host the Pittsburgh Pirates, Kevin found exactly what he needed and so did Kim Reedeaux.

Kim Reedeaux, upon botching her tryout camp attempt, had returned to Pittsburgh and to her staff position at KDKA radio. She may have been the morning sports anchor for the radio station, but resulting from her brief moment in the Cubs limelight, she had always flown to broadcast the Cubs-Pirates series in Chicago. She had made the trip for every Chicago-based Pirates series since she took over her father's radio program and did so, in a way, to honor his life-long love for the Cubs. Of course, as a broadcaster in the Pittsburgh market, her emphasis on the air had to be support for the Pirates franchise. Deep in Kim's heart, however, she was never saddened when a Cub pitcher struck out the side or the "W" flag flew atop Wrigley Field after the Cubbies had proven victorious against her hometown Pirates.

In the early morning hours of July 14, 2005, Kim Reedeaux arrived at Midway Airport in Chicago. The Pirates, a team in the middle of a terrible, mid-season spiral, were nine games below .500 with a record of 39–48. The franchise had hoped that the second half of the season, beginning with this four-game, weekend series with the Cubs, would lead to brighter days and better play. The Pittsburgh media had hoped for a change, too, but no one, including Kim, could foresee the "change" that would soon occur.

In the history of Major League Baseball, there had been many times when a brilliant athlete shined amid the atrocity that had befallen his team. During the 2005 season, the Pittsburgh Pirates had such a player in centerfielder Diego Lorenza. Diego, a young prodigy from Panama, had two brilliant traits that set him apart from the other athletes on his Pirates team. He had the capability of leaping for high-flies with the agility of a ballet dancer, turning his opponents' near-certain home run shots into certain outs. Diego was also a skillfully patient batter, an attribute uncommon among new Major Leaguers. Despite their woeful start to the 2005 season, the die-hard fans of the Pirates flocked to Pittsburgh's PNC Park – and any of the team's road venues – in order to support Diego Lorenza.

Kim Reedeaux was especially excited about the upcoming series between the Pirates and Cubs, not only because of Diego's talent, but also because of the imminent trade rumors that had been circulating about Diego moving to Chicago's North Side. Diego Lorenza was talented, no question, but with his talent came an ego. With his ego, came a hefty salary. For weeks, the Pittsburgh talk radio circuit had been abuzz with chatter about trading Diego. The reasons, given by fans, ranged from Diego's talent being too strong for such a weak franchise to trading him solely because he appeared to be outgrowing what the small market atmosphere could provide. The arguments were sound on both sides of the spectrum, but in any event, it was the upper management's call.

Whenever a star athlete is a member of a franchise, however mediocre or great a team's performance, the media personnel affiliated with the ball club in question must create classic quips to pique fan interest. From Harry Caray's trademark "Holy Cow," to Jack Brickhouse's standard "Hey, Hey," every broadcaster who had ever made a name for himself in sports had an edge – one call that set them apart from all the other sportscasters of the time.

For Kim Reedeaux, the call was, "With a hop, skip, and a jump, the batter is on second." The call was created specifically for Diego Lorenza because of his knack for hoping, skipping, and jumping his way around the base paths or to the outfield wall. The line had become the catch-phrase of Kim's broadcasts. KDKA-AM radio fans even had T-shirts printed with the words. Over the course of the third weekend in July of 2005, Kim's trademark phrase would change her life.

The game began under skies so clear that from the rooftops of the buildings surrounding Wrigley Field, one could turn away from the stadium and see the far banks of Lake Michigan. The weather was pleasantly mild for an early summer afternoon and despite the Pirates' woeful record, Kim looked from the press box and noticed many of the Bucs' brethren in attendance. By all rights, that day should have been just like all other days at Wrigley. That day was much different. Kim had been asked to sing, "Take Me Out to the Ballgame," a ritual begun by late-Cub broadcaster, Harry Caray, and continued after his death by celebrities and special invitees who arrived to serenade. The serenades, rarely in the best musical key, were still loved by the fans that lived and breathed the game of baseball. Of course, Kim was nervous; she knew that her singing ability was less than par and that the broadcast would be carried by hundreds, if not thousands, of television markets. However, Kim was sure that the intensity of the intra-division contest would keep her focused and calm her nerves. After all, her first priority was not her singing; it was providing a quality broadcast that Pittsburgh radio fans could follow and, in a way, feel the game as the action progressed.

The game started slowly for the Pirates. The Cubs' star, Jasper Richey, fanned the first three batters on seven pitches and unfortunately for the Bucs, Pittsburgh pitcher Ramon Dominguez was not as keen. By the bottom of the second inning, the score was 6–0 Cubs and Pittsburgh manager Lee Michaels was signaling for a lefty from the bullpen.

It becomes paramount, in a situation such as this, for the losing team's radio broadcaster to dazzle the listener for the sake of keeping them interested. That avenue was Kim's strong suit and she was armed and ready; she had learned from the best.

"With two out in the bottom of the second, the Cubs will send Pedro Marshall to the plate," Kim began. "Pedro has a .345 lifetime average against Richey; let us see what he can do here. Richey releases, Marshall connects and 'with a hop, skip, and a jump,' Pedro reaches second."

"With a hop, skip, and a jump" – Kim's trademark line – was used so energetically during a difficult spot for Pittsburgh fans. What she did not know, at that particular moment, was that WGN-Radio's General Manager, Kevin Geoffen, had been listening to the car radio while returning to the Pittsburgh airport after attending a regional sales meeting and knew he had his girl. Kim held every quality that he had wanted in a replacement for Les Williamson. She exuded grace, poise, and a knowledge base that few female play-by-play announcers had ever held. Kim was wise, yet shrewd when warranted, and she had played the game, albeit for one brief moment, several years earlier. For those reasons, alone, Kevin knew he had found his man, or I should say...girl. As the game progressed, Kevin Geoffen could not wait to arrive in Chicago to speak with Kim. Kim, likewise, could not wait to silently celebrate that certain Cubs victory. Victorious the Cubs proved to be that game, winning the contest by a score of 7–2. Yet, the true victor on that day soon proved to be Kim Reedeaux, the broadcaster – who had survived her singing effort with no ill effect.

Kim's stamina and layoff from the game may have dealt her a rough hand, but her skillfulness as an announcer and positive attitude toward her team and the sport had brought her back home to the Cubs again. Kim agreed to stay with the Pirates for the remainder of the 2005 broadcast season, prior to returning to Chicago and becoming the new voice of the Cubs for WGN Radio. Her pathway back to the Cubs, however, was only just beginning.

CHAPTER 17

"Good Afternoon, Everyone," Kim began, "it is time – yet again – for another exciting season of Chicago Cubs baseball." With that note, the Cubs' 2006 home baseball season began, as did Kim's career as a Cubs' broadcaster. Beginning in January, that year, the Cubs' previews started, but instead of critiquing the team's possibilities for the season, more sportswriters chose to predict how Kim, the "female," "the vixen," and the "one plate appearance wonder," would succeed as a broadcaster in the Chicago market. The criticism extended beyond the ivy-covered walls of Wrigley and far from the inner circle of proud baseball shaggers – the loyal fans who stood in the streets around the ballpark, awaiting their shot at glory and a coveted Cubs home run ball. Online analysts posted polls and opened many a chat session questioning how long Kim would last. Kim, however, just as determined as she had been over her entire life and career; knew she had the talent, skill, and strength to last the entire 162-game season and beyond. Kim may have joined the WGN radio team from Pittsburgh, but her support was clear: she was a Cub, at heart and by profession.

Kim was not concerned about her broadcast critics. Critics thrive in all facets of society. To her, having a critic merely meant she was well-known and doing her job as proficiently as she possibly could. She knew no one is satisfied with his or her job or choices 100% of the time. If they claimed to be, they'd be lying. Humans are fallible and no one is faultless. Kim never claimed to be the "diamond in the rough," but she had always stood up for herself when wronged. She had firmly stood by her innocence during the corked bat incident and she would stand up for herself against her critics, too. And, she did.

By 4:15 p.m., the ballgame – and Kim's first Cubs' broadcast – was over. The Northsiders had won the game 5–1 over the St. Louis Cardinals. The 40,869 fans in attendance were in mid-season form, as energetic in their cheers and screams as though the Cubs were deep in the N.L. Central Division race. From the new bleachers installed in the off-season, countless fans bowed as though to signify their never-ending praise for the Cubs religion.

The long-documented, decades-long Cubs-Cardinals rivalry demonstrated the Cardinals' uncanny success against Chicago. In fact, it had become rare for the Cubs to stand a chance in the series and fans of the Cardinals had often become a little belligerent about their team's success. Yet, this year was different; the Cub fan knew it and Kim did, too. There were some, of course, who argued that such positive thinking was typical of the Cub fan. I could not argue with them. I, too, have found myself – on many occasions – celebrating the beginning of another hopeful season in April, only to be waiting for "next year" by late September. This is something that speaks volumes about the uncertainty of baseball. A team that knew total dominance in the previous season or marked a highly successful winning ratio in Spring Training can just as easily be a "cellar dweller" by each new season's conclusion. The Cubs had proven the fact, many times over, and most recently during the 2003 and 2004 seasons. Still, there was something magical in the Lake Michigan–cooled air during April 2006. No one knew, then, what was so thrilling but something was captivating the Cub fan. That something – or someone – was Kim Reedeaux.

By 5 o'clock that Opening Day at Wrigley, the stadium was nearly empty. The fans whether by foot, by train, or by car, had made their way beyond Wrigleyville and went back to their normal lives. Some headed to Harry Caray's or another post-game mecca, known to the non-baseball fan as the neighborhood pub, where certainly the art of hindsight would present itself, time and again. Even in Cub victories, someone is always unhappy. Pitchers are caught yawning, making fans think the hurler did not care about the team; third basemen alley-oop sure-fire outs, allowing runners to reach base and score (as was the case that day). Again, no one – especially no baseball fan – is happy all of the time. Yet, as the fans filtered to the places where they would deliver the post-game recaps or "confessionals" to their priest – the bartender or fellow baseball nut that seemed willing to listen – Kim exited the press box and headed toward her car. Once inside, Kim keyed the ignition and heard the wonderful sounds of a long-lost favorite: "Go Cubs Go." Kim leaned back in her seat, smiled, and knew what she had to do. She knew she had to make one more comeback to the Big Leagues as a player. She vowed, then and there, to make it happen.

That night, Kim went home and called her boyfriend, Jeff, who was still living in Pittsburgh, to share her comeback decision. Jeff laughed at her and said, "Oh, get real Kim. April Fools' Day was last week. You're thirty-three years old; you'll be thirty-four this year. It's over, finished, done. You need to accept it and move on." Move on. Kim did and she did so without Jeff, whom she dumped soon after his suggestion that she let go of her dream. A relationship without support is not a healthy one at all. Jeff was not the only person to think Kim was crazy, but Kimberly Reedeaux was never one to let others' opinions hold her back. She defied the norm and she succeeded by doing so. She always had, so why would this effort be any different?

The next morning, Kim awoke at 5:00 a.m. and sensed something was wrong. She had no feeling in her left wrist. She wondered if she had slept crookedly or if, somehow, this was God's way of telling her that Jeff was right and her dream was crazy, given her advancing age. Kim needed to be at the ballpark by 9:00 a.m. for Game 2 of the Cubs-Cardinals series, but she wasn't sure if she could even turn her doorknob. She called Doug Darby, her WGN Radio color analyst, and asked him if he could cover the game day broadcast preparations while she visited her doctor. Kim was not one to take chances, especially when she was silently planning a return to the game.

En route to the doctor, with the feeling in her wrist restored, a pained Kim listened to the talk radio commentary of the previous day's home opener. Most of the callers, however, wanted to discuss her. Some were complimentary of her calls and highlighted her skills, both behind the microphone and on the field. More fans than not focused on ignoring her broadcasting abilities, choosing to instead rehash the corked bat incident. Because of that incident alone, they felt she could not be trusted. Despite the fact that she was innocent of the corking offense, some sports fans never let go of such things. To this day, Sammy Sosa is many fans' enemy #1 because he walked out on the Cubs' organization during the last game of the 2005 season. Kim did not care about popular, though. She did not enter the business to make friends; she entered the business to make a difference.

By the time she arrived at the doctor's office, Kim was more determined than ever to return to the game. Kim was like that. The more people condemned her efforts, the more inclined she was to pursue them, just to make a believer from a naysayer. First, however, was the doctor's appointment and Kim was stunned by what she heard. "You have carpal tunnel and need surgery, NOW."

The carpal tunnel diagnosis was not a life-or-death ordeal, but it posed a serious setback to Kim's plans for a rapid baseball return. The surgical recovery time would likely be a couple of months and she certainly could not throw during that time. A typical four-to-six-week setback, post-surgery, would mean that the earliest Kim could start returning to baseball form was mid-June to early-July and likely too late for the 2006 baseball season. Kim was very intelligent, though – intelligent enough to have scored 1500 on her SAT exam, to have excelled at both Northwestern University and the University of Notre Dame – schools known for their tough curriculum – and to have accomplished far more than anyone in her family or any woman in the world had ever accomplished. For one game, she had played with the boys of summer, as a regular season Major Leaguer.

Kim went home after the appointment, called her broadcast partner, and headed to Wrigley. As she witnessed the pregame festivities, she pondered her future. "To play or not to play" – that was the question, a question without a concrete answer. Kim had never been a quitter, she had always been a fighter, and it only took one small package, forwarded to her office, to convince her of the path she needed to pursue.

For many years, Kim had known that baseball is a rite of passage. Those who play the game have one or many God-given skills that few members of society will ever enjoy. The elite, blessed with such a gift, have two choices: to master the trade to the best of the individual's ability or to let the trade fade away as an underappreciated, if not unrealized, dream that countless others would die trying to know, even if for just one minute. Over the course of her life, Kim had lived the dream. She had beaten the odds, the critics, and time to achieve something marvelous. No, she had not found great baseball acclaim, but instead a heart purer than gold. As she stared at the letter resting in her palm, she remembered the past. She remembered a day, eons ago – or so it then seemed – and the little girl she would never forget. Anna Merkel, the young cancer patient that Kim had met when she was just a senior in high school, the bold and brave six-year-old whose infectious smile and will to survive had become such an inspiration. Why, sixteen years after Anna's passing, would her mom contact Kim, out of the blue? The answer was simple. She wanted to honor her daughter's last request.

Kim sat in her office, stared at the package for a few moments, and thought of Anna, the sweet little girl she had grown to love, all those years ago. The beautiful child who had so innocently held a baseball when Kim had met her; the little girl too honest to take something that was not hers; the princess that the "angels" called home much too soon. Kim opened the package carefully, her pained hand nearly shaking from the uncertainty of the small unit's contents. A small note card, addressed to Kim, and a cube surrounded in red and yellow tissue paper rested inside the box. Kim set the card aside for a few moments and began tearing away the tissue paper, which revealed something that stole Kim's breath. A baseball nestled safely within a shiny new protection cube – the very baseball that Kim had signed for the little girl that day at the pizzeria in Brentwood, so long ago.

As she wiped away tears, Kim made her way to the note card and wondered why Anna's mother had chosen to return the ball nearly two decades after her daughter's passing. The answer was soon clear. The little girl's dying wish had been for Kim to take that "special baseball" and win a big game for the angels. Kim knew what Anna had meant and deep in her heart, she believed the girl's dying wish was sweet. In keeping with her somewhat humorous mindset, Kim's first thought was "The Los Angeles Angels of Anaheim." Kim Reedeaux: always the consummate baseball lover.

For the rest of the day, Kim smiled when she thought of Anna, her dying wish, and her mother's testament to unending love by reaching out, those many years later. Yet, Kim knew she was facing surgery and an uncertain future for her return to the sport. With pen in hand and a legal pad on the desk, Kim was nearly ready to thank Sophie Merkel for the message and the ball. She had chosen her words carefully and pondered exactly what to say. She had resigned herself to needing surgery and thus, baseball was likely a dream she would never realize again. Kim clicked her pen top, and then moved her hand towards the paper. Something made her stop. Something cried out to Kim, "Don't do it." With an odd feeling within her heart Kim picked up the note card Sophie had sent, yet again. This time, however, she noticed some writing on the back. The writing, dictated by a young girl with very youthful, yet treasured thoughts, moved Kim to tears. The message was a poem that simply said:

Mommy said that love is a day in the sun,
A hot dog with ketchup, a burger and bun;
But, I say that love is that big pickle jar
at the park where Kim is the superstar.

Kim could hardly contain her feelings. She had never realized the magnitude of the impact she made on Anna or anyone else's life, through her love of baseball. Anna's innocent and beautiful view of their friendship proved to Kim how important her dream was to others. She had helped a little girl's final months seem brighter and she still longed to do the same for others. From beyond her grave, little Anna Merkel had, once again, taught Kim a lesson. Anna showed Kim that friendship is worth its weight in gold, love is everlasting, and dreams are worth the fight for reaching them. Anna's dreams never got that chance to be reached; Kim's had been and could be again. Knowing this made one baseball player's decision regarding her future quite easy. Kim was ready to "Play Ball."

Whether staring down a veteran southpaw pitcher or an unwitting surgeon, Kim Reedeaux had a knack for intimidating people. Maybe it was her charismatic way or her "never accept defeat" attitude, but regardless of the reason behind it, Kim knew how to turn heads.

The morning of Kim's carpal tunnel surgery was no exception. Kim arrived at South Oak Harbor Medical Center at 6:45 a.m. Nearly two weeks had passed since she decided to give her baseball dream another chance and while most people view surgery with regret or trepidation, Kim viewed this surgery as a small setback in a dream she was destined to live. Of course, as with any surgical procedure, there was risk, but Kim was used to risks. It was a risk to challenge her high school for their unequal treatment of girls and boys athletics. It had been another threat to challenge Major League Baseball and its long-withstanding policies. Kim accepted risk and felt no risk was too great. The rewards, reaped by challenging risk, were simply too enticing; the rewards could lead to a dream come true.

By day's end, Kim's surgery was complete and had been as flawless as Kim's return to the Majors, a mere twenty-eight months later, would be. The dream was no longer just hers; she needed to return to baseball for Anna, her special angel whose dreams she could fulfill.

CHAPTER 18

"It's a very simple game." Douglas Drubalm, catcher of the 2008 Cubs, quipped. "You throw the ball; you catch the ball; you hit the ball." Twenty years earlier, those words had been uttered in the movie *Bull Durham* and yet, two decades later, the sentiments pertained to the Cubs. The 2008 season marked the beginning of a monumental year for the little ball club on the Windy City's north side. Often the victims of Major League tragedy, the Cubs were coming off postseason disappointment, having won the N.L. Central title the previous September, only to be swept 3–0 in the NLDS. More importantly – at least to the team's critics – the 2008 Cubs' season marked a century since the club had last uttered the words, "World Champions." The stakes were high. During the 2007 Winter Meetings, the Cubs had lost their shortstop to free agency and were placing their hopes, dreams, and season on a young rookie named Juan Marco Mendoza.

A Cuban refugee, Juan Marco had escaped the long arm of Castro and survived a cold, lonely trip aboard a tiny raft made of bamboo. He landed in freedom on the sands of Miami in November 1995. Just fifteen years old when he arrived, Juan had left his entire family in Cuba. He came to America with the clothes on his back and a dream. After years in the Minor Leagues, his dream was coming true on a field were many dreams were cast – the hallowed grounds of Wrigley Field.

While Juan was beginning his Major League dream, a woman whose life had been a dream throughout, Kim Reedeaux, was preparing for her first game of the 2008 Minor League season. Once again a Minor League sensation and fully recovered from her carpal tunnel setback, Kim had worked her way to the Cubs Triple-A affiliate in Iowa. She had recovered more quickly and in better form than many expected, but Kim had beaten the odds since birth. She began her daily workout program in October 2006, six months after her surgery, signed with Single-A Peoria in the spring of 2007 and was once more set to lead the

Iowa Cubs to greatness – while her own plans for greatness stayed within reach.

Of course, Kim was still the victim of critics. The critics who cringed over her role as a WGN-Radio broadcaster and suggested she would not last a season soon, candidly, expressed their "rightness" as Kim resigned her position to continue her baseball journey as a player. Kim also met critics, yet again, during her stints in Single-A and Double-A. None of that mattered. Kim was committed and no one was going to steal that. She had committed her dream not only to her family and self, but also to the Markel's. Kim longed to make little Anna's last wish a reality.

For the first three months of the 2008 season, the Cubs looked to be unstoppable. By all accounts, the club emerged as a worthy candidate for eliminating the "goat curse" once and for all. The Cubs were nearly twenty games over .500 with a record of 50–33 by the end of June. Then, tragedy stuck. Through nearly half the baseball season, Juan Marco Mendoza proved why he had overcome the odds and made it to the Major Leagues. He led the Majors in RBIs, held a .378 batting average, a .402 on-base percentage, and mustered a team record of twenty-one home runs through June. He appeared to be a surefire Gold Glove Award candidate by the season's end because of his spectacular defense as well.

Mendoza's success and the revelation he would likely win the season's Gold Glove award was somewhat poetic in nature. For Mendoza, winning the award would validate his choice to leave his family for following his dream; for the baseball fan and historian, the trophy would bring the Cubs something that the organization had not seen since 1970, a Gold Glove winner at shortstop. The last Cubs' Gold Glover at the shortstop position, Don Kessinger, won the award twice in the back to back years of 1969 and 1970. The doubters of the Cubs – and Mendoza – turned to one thing and one thing only when considering the potential of a rookie Gold Glover – the club's Gold Glove history at short and more specifically, the team's history in 1969. Kessinger was a part of the infamous 1969 Cubs' late season collapse that led the "Miracle Mets" of New York to World Series glory, shutting out the "close but wait 'til next year" Cubbies again.

As the 2008 season progressed, Mendoza's critics began to get the better of him. Strong-willed, Mendoza worked harder and practiced longer, sometimes practicing without adequate warm-up time. He wanted an extra edge. In the end, however, what Mendoza received, instead of an award for his greatness, was a season-ending injury: a ruptured left quadricep, sustained during his carelessness. Pleased to be a part of the "team" after having worked so hard to prove himself, Mendoza over-exerted himself, trying too hard to "help the club." His loyalty to the little baseball team on Chicago's North Side ultimately left his beloved team stranded without their "star" during what would prove to be a difficult period in the season. On paper, and despite Juan Marco's injury, the Cubs' record spoke for itself. The team had a record of 85–50 on the 29th day of August, halfway through a four-game home stand with the Philadelphia Phillies. But, the winds of change would soon be blowing, in more ways than one.

Mendoza's quad damage meant a two- to three-month healing period. Therefore, his stellar season was finished and the team was left without his solid fielding and high on-base percentage. As the fans or any lover of the sport would say, that's baseball and baseball can deal a cruel hand. Then again, sometimes, such instances in baseball are fate. Waiting in the wings was an up-and-coming thirty-six-year old who was no stranger to the game – Kim Reedeaux, who relished the opportunity to walk the hallowed grounds of Wrigley again.

It was the first day of September 2008. The Houston Astros were in Chicago to begin a three-game series at the Friendly Confines, during a time of turmoil within the Cubs organization. A team that had played so soundly all season, the Cubs were beginning to show signs of late summer fatigue. The club had allowed the Phillies to score five runs in each of the series' final two games to close the month of August. During those two games, the Cubs managed to score a total of only five runs. It was becoming evident that losing Mendoza's offensive abilities were catching up with the team. It was time to make a change, to shake up the team with a player who had been there before, someone who had been in tough situations and excelled. It was time for Kim Reedeaux.

Kim re-joined the Cubs' big league organization at Wrigley Field after the team's September 1, 2008, loss to the Houston Astros, which extended their losing streak to three games. According to media reports, Kim's return was meant to "shake up a team that had fallen asleep," but that wasn't entirely true. The Cubs were still sitting atop the National League's Central Division and nearly twenty games over .500. The club's early success in the 2008 season left some breathing room between the Cubs and their opponents. One losing streak didn't appear to make or break the franchise. In actuality, the organization decided that Kim had proven herself, through a memorable and record-setting Minor League season, and deserved the opportunity.

Indeed, the winds of change were in the air on many levels, short and long term. Most memorably, however, on a late October night, just six years later, those winds had brought Game 7 of the World Series – and a forty-two-year-old ballplayer's dream – to a screeching halt. With Kim's mind elsewhere – somewhere in the distance – she was quickly brought back to life with the words, "Ladies and gentlemen, we will resume play in fifteen minutes." On that note, Kim smiled and grabbed her bat.

CHAPTER 19

The ending of baseball's 2008 regular season brought another time for celebration in the little area known as Wrigleyville. For the second straight season, the Cubs won the N.L. Central Division title; again, they were playoff bound. "Would this be the year?" many fans asked themselves. Baseball fans across Chicago, despite their regular season loyalties, placed high hopes on the Cubs' postseason chances. By the season's homestretch, their division lead was insurmountable. This had to be the year, didn't it? All signs seemed to point to Cub greatness, to overcoming the past and the past season's "sweep" to end it without the coveted and long-sought Championship. If the saying, "Good things come to those who wait," was true, then the Cubs had waited a century for the title; the rest would simply fall into place, right? For the optimist, yes; in reality, the Cubs had proven, time and again, to never count your blessings too early for you'll set yourself up for heartbreak.

One place where heartbreak was not likely to resonate was within Kim Reedeaux's heart. The debut month in her storybook return to the Cubs had been nothing short of outstanding. She easily picked up the pieces left by the injury to Juan Pablo Mendoza. In just one month of play, Kim had notched five homers and knocked in twenty runners during the team's last twenty-two games. As a result, Kim Reedeaux became the first woman to ever win the National League's coveted "Rookie of the Month" award. For Kim and the Cubs, their hard work was just beginning. In baseball, Spring Training seems like an appetizer, a sample of the season to come; the regular season is a savory dinner of 162 different dishes; but the postseason is the much awaited and anticipated dessert that every baseball franchise longs to save room for and enjoy. Having made their way into the postseason, the Cubbies were faced with greater challenges. The checklist included beating the Los Angeles Dodgers, advancing beyond the Division Series to the N.L. Championship Series — where the club had not been since 1989; reaching the World Series, for the first time since 1945, and winning the

World Championship, the first in a century. What better year to win the Championship than the century mark from when the title was last claimed by the franchise?

The momentary quiet time, prior to the postseason's first showdown with the Dodgers, brought brief moments of reflection. Soon, however, everything became strictly business. The Dodgers, busy in the 2007 offseason, had hired a new manager and brought several new faces to their 2008 roster and coaching staff. Despite the changes, the Los Angeles team clinched the N.L. West title with a regular season record of 84–78. To the new baseball fan, this matchup may have seemed a little inequitable: a team whose manager in his first season with a new ball club, against the Cubs with a much better record. The matchup was anything but unbalanced. The Cubs' and Dodgers' respective skippers were seasoned veterans who had not only managed several World Series winning clubs over the years but were also former players. From the managerial standpoint, the NLDS appeared to be a statistical dead heat. The teams were also fairly equal in offense and defense. There was not much for the fan to base the series' projections on, other than the past and even that was not the best guide. The Cubs' record in the postseason noted the team's misfortunes, but the Dodgers had not won a postseason series in twenty years. Again, to the seasoned sports fan, it looked as though the division series would be a well-matched, close affair. Little did Cub fans know, however, that heartache would again be their calling card.

The 2008 NLDS between the Dodgers and Cubs began at Wrigley Field on October 1, and the date had not been kind to the Wrigleyville faithful in the past. It was on October 1, 1934, that the oft unlucky Cubbies dropped both games of a double-header with the Pittsburgh Pirates to fall out of the pennant race. Seventy-four years later, a woman from Pittsburgh — Kim Reedeaux – in her second tour of duty with the Cubs, was in the dugout, waiting and wondering if she'd be making her postseason debut. Kim did not start that night; however, the staff informed her that she could pinch hit in the later innings. She was ready and her chance to play would come earlier as the result of a third inning hamstring injury to the starter. Kim's readiness aside, she heard the sports radio banter about how much rode on this first game. Historically, thirty-eight of the fifty-six teams to win the NLDS's Game 1 went on to later win the Division Series. Winning isn't always everything, but for the long-suffering Cub fan and those that prided themselves on statistics, the little club on Chicago's North Side really needed to raise the "W" flag after Game 1.

The weather befitted the matchup. A cool night with relatively light winds welcomed the standing-room-only, over–regular-season capacity crowd of 42,000-plus. The carnival-like atmosphere of cheers and chatter that always came from cautiously optimistic Cub fans echoed from all the entrances and corners of the ballpark. The stands were a sea of Cubbie blue. Young children clung tightly to their "Addison" teddy bears; their mothers were adorned in their pink Cub hats or wrapped in their logo blankets; their fathers munched on Italian sausage and downed some suds, each fan with one dream in mind: advancement in the postseason. After all, with a 100- year World Series drought, taking the postseason one out, one inning, and one game at a time made the most sense.

The Dodgers' first inning went quickly with a strikeout, a walk, and a 6-4-3 double play. The Cubs' first inning was just as uneventful, leaving everyone in attendance to believe the game would either be the world's greatest defensive battle or a total bore. The back-and-forth baseball version of the Burr-Hamilton duel continued through the top of the second; after 1½ innings, no runs, hits, nor errors were notched. The bottom of the second for the Cubs looked dismal until the Cubs' star second baseman put a two-run homer on Waveland Avenue for the "fishing net faithful" to land. The stadium erupted; the Cubbies appeared to be on their way. Two runs on three hits in the inning gave the Cubs a 2–0 lead heading into the third, a lead that held through the Dodgers' next two frames.

In the top of the fifth, the Cubs pitching coach talked with their ace pitcher, who had shown visible signs of fatigue in the latter stages of the third inning. Begging—still largely the popular method that pitchers employ to state their reasons for staying in the game—ensued and the pitching coach decided to leave DeMuir in the game. The first batter grounded out to Kim at short. The next walked. The next flied out to right field. With two outs, it looked like DeMuir would escape. The next two batters walked and singled, leaving the bases loaded for the Dodgers' star. When Allen Ellsworth fell to a 0–2 count on the first two pitches, Cub Nation believed the lead would remain intact. DeMuir followed the 0–2 count with a slider dubbed a foul and a change-up called a ball before a pitch known as "The Disaster." The Disaster was a 92-mph fast ball, securely placed in Allen Ellsworth's sweet zone, which he ricocheted into the bleachers for a grand slam home run and a

Dodgers 4–2 lead. The fans, who had been so optimistic, nearly booed DeMuir off the field.

When pitching coach Randy Richmond did not remove Ellsworth from the game, the Northsiders' faithful followers in unison uttered chants of terminating both him and the pitcher on the spot. The Curse was intact, yet again – or was it just bad play? I choose to believe the latter.

The Dodgers added three more runs off the Cubs relief core, one apiece in the seventh, eighth, and ninth innings to win the postseason opener 7–2. As history showed, the Cubs did not recover, losing the N.L. Division series in a three games to none sweep. The World Series drought would move past 100 years. With the heart of Wrigleyville despondent over the loss, Kim Reedeaux found herself to be a mixed bag of emotions – happy to be playing ball, sad to heading home before her team's wish came true.

CHAPTER 20

When asked how he handled the baseball offseason, Rogers Hornsby said that he "stared out the window and waited for spring." This philosophy rings true not only for the baseball player but also the fan. The truest baseball fan can tell you the number of days until pitchers and catchers report at any given time during the winter months. They follow the Winter Meetings and watch replays on the MLB Network to get their fix of balls and strikes until the dark season returns to light. Spring Training may give no true insight at all for how the upcoming season will be, but fans flock to the stadiums when the first week of March arrives, unable to contain their baseball-less "cabin fever" any longer. In 2009, the Cubs' Spring Training facility in Arizona, Hohokam Park, set a single-season attendance record of over 203,000 fans for nineteen home dates. One of the fans that witnessed the Cubs' .500 spring of nineteen wins and nineteen losses was Jeremy Borgia.

Raised in the rural village of Cherish, Ohio, Jeremy "cherished" only one thing: the Chicago Cubs. A computer geek by profession, he spent his entire life trying to claw his way through friendships, relationships, and small town chatter as a Cub fan in heavily loyal Cincinnati Reds' country. He could not eat at the one restaurant in town when a game was on; everything was "Reds," "Reds," "Reds." Even one church service in town concluded with "And Lord pray for our beloved Reds during this season. May they stay safe, healthy, and bring the title home." It was – to play on a movie title – "No country for Old Cub fans." Jeremy was not old, but his love for old-time baseball and the hapless hundred years of Cub shortfalls rang true.

During the first decade of the twenty-first century, finding career success in a weak economy – especially in rural America – proved quite the struggle. When Jeremy's company gave him the opportunity to advance his career and move to Las Vegas in late 2008, needless to say, he took it. The monetary benefit played a huge role in his choice to move but there was another reason: Cubs Spring Training in Las Vegas.

Each year, the Cubs travel to "Sin City" one weekend of their Spring Training tour. He vowed to be in the stands for that weekend.

On March 27, 2009, Jeremy walked into Cashman Field in Las Vegas with front-row tickets he nabbed from an internet auction, grabbed a program and some popcorn, and settled in for some split-squad action between the Cubs and the White Sox. Of all the players he wanted to see – Soriano, Ramirez, Lee, etc. – he wanted to see Reedeaux the most. Yes, Kim. He wanted to see "the girl," "the vixen," "the publicity stunt," or whatever else the sportswriters chose to call her. Jeremy found himself fascinated by her in ways he could not explain. He hung on her every throw and at-bat, not in a way that a stalker would – he assured his buddies that he was too mesmerized by her talent to be harmful – but in the way that an appreciative fan would honor his baseball hero – or in this case – heroine. Would some call his "admiration" for Kim bizarre? Sure, in the eyes of some. He bought everything with her picture on it he could get his hands on: baseball cards, magazines, etc. He had the shirts, hats, and other novelty items created after her Rookie-of-the Month award win the previous year. He launched an online blog for fellow "Kim's Kubs." Yet; he was just a loyal fan – maybe the most loyal fan – that Kim Reedeaux had. He convinced himself this "love" for Kim was normal.

Given how loyal a fan Jeremy was, it would be easy to see why he was heartbroken that Kim was not in the lineup for the game. Maybe upset is too mild a word or maybe he was more stalker-like than he claimed. He caused a scene screaming, "Kim should be playing. Something's wrong with this picture. This team sucks and they want to lose. She's the star. The rest of you are losers. I bleed Cubbie Blue; you'uns bleed black, you black hearted…" Well, you can probably figure out the last word in the outburst.

Jeremy's misconstrued over-exuberance upset nearby fans and had security ready to escort him from the premises until Jeremy agreed to settle down and behave. A member of the coaching staff came from the dugout and spoke with Jeremy, explaining that Kim had made the Opening Day roster, but the manager chose to give her a rest day that Friday night.

Dean Dawson, bench coach, walked over to where Jeremy sat and said, "Son, we're sorry that your favorite player, Ms. Reedeaux, is not playing tonight, but you must understand that she needs to rest to be ready for Opening Day."

Jeremy nodded in agreement and Dawson continued, "We thank you for your outpouring of support for the team and hope that you watch for Kim on your TV or in person all season."

Jeremy again nodded. For the 13,226 other fans in attendance that night, such an explanation and props for being a fan would have sufficed, but not for Jeremy. He needed to see Kim, even if he didn't believe his obsession was a problem.

Kim Reedeaux was many things: a daughter, a sister, a niece, an aunt, a college graduate, a sportscaster, and a baseball player. Most of all, Kim carried a special warmth in her heart for the baseball fan. The Cubs' coaching staff debated whether or not to tell Kim about the obsessed fan that longed to see her. They did not know how she – or better yet, he – would react. Kim overheard the coaches' discussion, walked up to them, and said, "You guys can be honest with me. What's up?"

"Kim, we have a situation in the stands," Coach Dawson explained.

"Oh?"

"Yes. There's a man, obviously a little off, who seems obsessed with you that is voicing his displeasure with your off day today."

"Let me go and see him," Kim begged.

"I don't think that's a good idea," Dawson and three other coaches replied in unison.

"Well, Mr. Dawson, no disrespect, but our coaching staff didn't think putting in a reliever for the fifth inning of our last game of last year made sense either. I'm going." Kim grabbed a baseball and walked from the dugout toward the tearful, obsessed fan.

"Hi!" Kim said, as if no weirdness had ever occurred, "I'm Kim Reedeaux and I understand you're a fan."

Jeremy seemed stunned that she was standing before him, only able to utter a meek, "Uh-huh."

"Here. Catch," Kim said, as she tossed him a signed baseball. "Enjoy the game and be sure to come out and see me play at Wrigley sometime."

Jeremy didn't even know what to say. Kim's coaches didn't either, but she handled the situation in a cool, calm and collected fashion, like a pro, even if Kim did not tell them about inviting him to Chicago. To Kim, there was no threat; Jeremy was just an over-excitable fan. She'd seen them; she'd been there.

When the game began, the drama ended. The Cubs came out of the gate swinging and notched seven runs before the first inning ended. They added two more runs in the fourth and won the game 9-4. The obsessed fan from Cherish, Ohio, enjoyed many things that day. He witnessed a Cubs victory, despite Kim's off day. He lived every fan's dream to sit in the stands, yell for his team, and leave the game with a sense of fulfillment having relived a small piece of the past. Besides the victory, Jeremy secured something he'd cherish forever – a Kim Reedeaux–signed baseball and one moment that would live forever in time and his memory, or, at least one moment until he could make it to Chicago. He could not wait to blog about it.

"Guess What I Did?" read the headline on the "Kim's Kubs" blog on the morning of March 31, 2009. Jeremy posted a photo of the baseball Kim signed and of course, fudged the details about the day. He couldn't let his "public" know that he was obsessed or insane. His blog followers, nearly all 200 of them, posted smiley faces. Some said, "You so Photoshopped that picture." Some said, "Big deal." Some said, "Kudos." And one said, "Did you take her back to your hotel?" The latter, to a twisted mind like Jeremy's, seemed like a brilliant idea but realistically, the whole world knew he stood no chance. After all, Kim, over the off-season, had begun dating Bradley James, a precious metals trader and Chicago native with ties to the Pittsburgh area who looked a little like Clark Kent and treated her like royalty. Bradley was everything in her life that Jeff, her unsupportive ex-boyfriend, had not been, and everything that, despite his efforts, Jeremy Borgia could never be.

The start of the Cubs' 2009 season began in Houston for a series against the Astros. As always for an Astros' home opener, there was a street festival with prize patrols from Houston area radio stations in front of Minute Maid Park handing out prizes to radio and baseball fans. Whenever the Cubs came to Houston, one thing was clear, whether you attended the game live or watched on television: Cub fans always arrive to the game early; Astros fans sometimes roll in around the second inning. The reasons are still unknown, other than that Cub fans are loyal, no matter where they are. The atmosphere at Minute Maid Park that April day was electric, and Kim hoped the fire that night would extend to her bat.

As the stadium disc jockey, loyal to the Astros team and known for posting the occasional "Cubs Suck" message via his social media presence, cranked out a series of up-tempo tunes spanning genres from Metallica to Muse and Pearl Jam to Paramore, the crowd settled in for the start of the season. For the Cub faithful in Houston, the 2009 hopefulness was clear very early.

Alfonso Soriano led off the first inning with a home run. Ramirez followed with a solo shot of his own in the second inning. Kim hit an RBI late in the game and the Cubs won the opener, 4–2. Cub fans immediately began talking about how "Next Year is Now"; the Houston sportswriters and radio jocks were not as confident. After all, it had been 101 seasons since the Cubs won it all. It was easy to understand the skepticism.

By the 2009 All-Star Break, the Cubs were a .500 ball club. Injuries plagued the team for most of the spring and Kim had not been immune. She missed most of the spring with a shoulder injury and became injured again soon after her return. Of course, the skeptics said the Cubs' record validated their early season views; the Cubs' fans chalked up the difficulties to the injury bug. Regardless, if the Cubs were going to win anything, their season's second half needed to be far better than the first.

The month of July held much promise. The team won two-thirds of their games and ended the month seven games over .500. The on-field excitement was short-lived. Despite scoring seventeen runs against Kim's hometown Pittsburgh Pirates in the middle of August, the Cubs finished the season's fifth month back at .500 ball and dealt with drama behind the scenes as Jeremy Borgia came to Chicago with one goal in mind: to make the "hot" Kim Reedeaux his.

CHAPTER 21

Not since 1949, when ex-Chicago Cub Eddie Waitkus dealt with an obsessed fan that could have cost him his life, had such a case of severe infatuation affected baseball. Never before had stalking impacted a female in the league. There was no other female in the league, just Kim. Waitkus, similar to Kim, began his Major League career with the Cubs and showed great promise until a fan's obsession impacted everything. Sixty years later, that fan was Jeremy Borgia – the unglued Spring Training admirer who, despite his efforts to convince the world he was harmless, became sicker and sicker every day.

Kim missed more of the 2009 season than she played. The injury-driven off-time allowed her to grow closer to her sweetheart, Bradley, and she gave no further thought to that day in Las Vegas or the guy she told to "see her play" in Chicago. She gave no thought to Borgia until pictures of Bradley and Kim in their apartment arrived in the mail. She immediately contacted police.

"Does anyone you know have a grudge against you, Ms. Reedeaux?" Sergeant David Oates of the Chicago PD asked the young star.

"I don't know," Kim said.

"How about your teammates; any trouble there?"

"Not that I can think of."

"Neighbors…fans…"

Kim stopped the sergeant. "I did have an issue during Spring Training in Las Vegas, but surely this wouldn't be…" Kim confessed.

"Tell us about that," Oates said, attentively listening to her every word.

Kim told him about the encounter, her handling of it and how she had innocently told him to come to Chicago for a game. Two things soon followed: Jeremy Borgia became a person of interest in the apparent case of stalking and Kim Reedeaux got a restraining order against Borgia, just in case. Even in the case of the ostensible stalking,

Kim faced critics. Some said she brought it on herself or that she should forget it and move on. Others said this was a good time for her to quit the sport. More still said that her personal matters should not interfere with the day-to-day operations of the Cubs organization or else they would stop supporting her. How sad that an ill individual targeted a young woman because of an obsession with her talent and others chose only to blame her! Unfortunately, the statistics on the topic of blaming the victim are as alarming as those on stalking itself.

With a restraining order granted, Kim felt safer. However, she soon realized that restraining orders for stalking are not always effective and Borgia found alternative means of bothering Kim. When he could not contact her, he trashed her good name on internet message boards, his blog, other baseball blogs, and he did so in ways that would make even the toughest person's stomach feel queasy. While there are two sides to every story and the fans did not know Kim's side – aside from the fans that witnessed the outburst in Las Vegas – they judged her by believing what Borgia posted about her. Every comment Borgia posted, mind you, was a figment of his illness or imagination but far too many people ignored the premise of "Don't ever totally believe what you read."

By the time of the roster expansion at the first of September 2009, the torment Kim endured off the field made its way to the field and began to impact her ability to play the game. The unhappy fans' calls for Kim to take a leave of absence, quit the team, or be demoted to the Minors echoed, as the fans longed to blame anything for the fact the Cardinals were atop the Central Division. Scandal seemed to be a better focal point than their N.L. Central second place position. Second place to a long-suffering Cub fan is never acceptable practice.

After a 6–4 victory over the Cincinnati Reds on 9/11, Kim looked toward the Chicago Board Options Exchange (CBOE) seats and saw Jeremy Borgia. She briefly glanced at him, hoping he would not see her. Unfortunately, he not only saw Kim but made a threatening hand gesture. As quickly as an outfielder running backwards to catch a ball headed for the bleachers, Kim said, "Enough." She walked off the field, went into the locker room, packed her stuff and said, "I'm done." For the second time in Kim's life, she vowed to quit baseball.

When Kim arrived home from the ballpark, she walked into the most beautiful scene imaginable. Rose petals stretched from the front doorstep to the kitchen. In the kitchen, Kim found a homemade heart-shaped pizza and a note on the coffee pot, instructing her to walk to the patio. On the patio, she found more rose petals and a baseball that said, "You + Me = Forever. 9.11.09." On the other side of the ball, a simple note: "Will You Marry Me?" As Kim stared at the baseball with tears welling in her eyes, Bradley sneaked up behind her for a surprise hug.

"How was your day, Future Mrs. James?" Bradley confidently asked, sure she would say "Yes."

"Jeremy was at the game and I quit," Kim announced.

Bradley paused for a moment and then said, "Good?" He didn't know whether to be happy or sad.

"It's all good, future husband of mine. This is the only diamond I need," Kim said as she slipped the diamond on her finger and leaned in for another kiss. While happy, Bradley knew that Kim had just lied to him. He knew no amount of stalking could keep Kim Reedeaux from baseball. And it didn't for long, but not until after a challenge or three.

As Bradley and Kim began planning their wedding, it began looking more like one of David Letterman's "Top Ten" lists on the topic of "How Much Kim Reedeaux Needs Baseball Despite What She Says." The first decision the couple needed to make was choosing a date. Kim was quick to announce they could not marry in February because she wanted to follow the news from camp; March through October because of Spring Training and the season, optimistic to see the Cubs in the postseason again; or in early December because of the Winter Meetings. (But she was done with baseball.)

The second decision they had to make was their wedding venue, but focusing Kim on that when she spent every waking minute trying to determine how many different ways to incorporate baseball into her wedding (believe me, there are a ton if you think about it) was tough. At one point, Bradley said, "Why don't we marry at Wrigley?" Kim said, "Ugh, no! I'm tired of baseball." He said nothing and just rolled his eyes. Yes, the whole world could tell she was tired of baseball.

The third decision was largely non-baseball related. What should the newlyweds-to-be do about the stalker and his threats? Should they move from the area or stay and make their way through the struggle together? Laughing about it and blowing it off was no longer an issue. The harassment had become too serious. In the back of his mind, Bradley knew Kim loved baseball and never wanted to leave it, but a part of his inner psyche also believed she had become baseball bridezilla crazy as an escape from facing the reality, which became more apparent as the days' progressed.

Bradley never believed that Kim seriously wanted to walk away from the game that had been her life for a good percentage of it. He believed that about as much as he believed that money grew on trees. So when Kim tossed aside her diet and exercise program and began eating everything under the sun, he knew something was wrong. She wasn't pregnant; this much he knew for sure. The two had taken every precaution and used every birth control measure on the market to ensure that did not happen until they were ready. Kim was screaming on the inside, begging for a life raft. Until she was ready to accept it, however, there was not much that anyone could do.

One Thursday afternoon, Bradley came home from work on his lunch break and found Kim on the floor, curled up in the fetal position, crying.

"What's wrong, baby?" he asked, as he consoled her.

"Look," Kim said, pointing at a box in the corner of the room.

Inside the box was fifteen years of Kim's life, one clipping and autograph at a time, each one labeled with comments that no individual – victim, woman or otherwise – should ever read. For the next few weeks, Kim could not sleep; her eating habits changed; she could not stop crying; and she wanted to do none of the things that were once her routine, including Saturday "cheat night" pizza. It became apparent that she was suffering from a dose of depression at the very least and the love of her life was worried. Brad called her father.

A sleepy Harold Reedeaux received the phone call at 10:45 that Thursday night and with the words, "Mr. Reedeaux, it's Kim,…" he was suddenly wide awake. Over the course of the next hour, Bradley explained in full detail everything that had occurred with Kim's stalker and the methods the police used to stop it.

"Restraining orders don't always work, Brad." Harold said in a concerned voice. "She shouldn't have to hide forever."

Bradley explained that the cops were doing everything they could to prevent the torture.

"No one can protect her like I can," Harold said. "I'll pack a bag and begin driving that way tonight."

"You're not flying, Harold?" Bradley asked.

"No. I have an idea," Harold explained. He said nothing else, but Harold knew exactly how to stop this and get the message across to leave his baby girl alone.

After promising his wife that he would "take care of Kim's problem" without her, Harold hit the road at midnight. Angry and not thinking clearly as he planned his trip at that late hour, Harold chose the scenic route to Chicago, bypassing I-80 for I-70's more distant route. The nearly nine-hour, 557-mile drive from his front door to Kim's gave him ample opportunity to think about his daughter, her baseball journey, his love for her, and how he would protect her. Protection and some peace for Kim, in the form of a father's eternal love, was less than a day away.

CHAPTER 22

Harold Reedeaux arrived in Chicago as the early lunch traffic hit the outskirts of the Windy City. As he sat behind an accident on the Dan Ryan Expressway, he remembered a day, soon after Kim was born, when her beautiful smile had led him to announce that he'd be cleaning his hunting rifle if any man came near her, so the man would know he'd use it if Kim was ever hurt. Men had come near her over the years. Kim never knew harm, so her prior boyfriends did not either. Stalkers were a different story. Harold placed faith in law enforcement and opposed taking the law into his own hands. He'd never think of killing the stalker unless placed in a situation that required saving himself or his family from Mr. Borgia. No one in the world could blame him.

When Harold saw his daughter for the first time since the most recent stalking episode began, his heart broke. Kim's hair was a mess. It was obvious she had not slept well (she had bags under her eyes that could hold enough luggage for a Hawaiian honeymoon); the slightest noise from a car alarm siren or knock at the neighbors' door put her on edge. Harold's beautiful daughter was miserable and the stalking was making her sick.

"Mr. Reedeaux, do not worry," Officer Ben Plant said, while stationed outside Kim's home. "If criminals were smart, they would not commit crime. We WILL catch this guy."

Harold, spoken like a true sportscaster and dad, said, "When? After we have a redo of the Waitkus shooting?"

Officer Plant had no response. He sensed Harold's frustration and that disgust echoed Chicago PD's own. This guy was sneaky; he was clever; he had obviously stalked others before. He was a professional.

In time, all professional criminals are apprehended, even if ultimately through exhaustion, a need to be caught, or slip-ups. In the case of Jeremy Borgia, his number was up by that weekend's close.

After what was clearly a heavy night of drinking, Jeremy Borgia arrived at Kim's front door. Instead of Kim, he quickly met two plain-clothed Chicago police officers who read him his rights and hauled him downtown.

"I'm a Las Vegas resident. You can't do this. Kim loves me. She'll bail me out…" An entire neighborhood cheered when they saw Borgia seated in the patrol car, handcuffed. Kim simply cried; it warmed her heart that she was that loved by her neighbors. The terror, the torment, and the trauma were too much, but the nightmare was over and deep down, Kim was glad. She knew she was strong enough to heal.

For the next two days, Kim awoke only long enough to use the restroom and eat. Refreshed, Kim called the Cubs' Front Office and asked to take the rest of the season as a leave of absence. Her request granted, without question, Kim was still a Chicago Cub, stalker-free, and looking towards the future with her husband-to-be and family. On that note, she said, "Honey, how about a January 22 wedding?"

"January 22?" Bradley asked. "Is January free for you?"

Kim laughed, reflecting back to her "baseball bridezilla" moments.

"It's winter; it's Chicago; it'll snow…guaranteed, Kim. Really?"

"It won't snow in Arizona!" Kim screamed.

"Let's get married at Hohokam Park!"

Bradley knew he could never change her mind and deep down, he didn't want to change it.

Kim, Bradley, and her parents spent the rest of 2009 in Arizona, planning the happy couple's January 2010 nuptials, ensuring that everything would be done and squared away before pitchers and catchers reported in February.

So how do you plan a Chicago Cub–themed wedding in a little less than four months? Kim, frugal and down to earth, had only one answer: power shopping. She logged onto her computer and secured her Cubs-logo garter, baseball-themed flower arrangements, and favors from different online vendors. She contacted Larry Leopold, the Cubs' Spring Training chaplain, to conduct the ceremony. Each week she checked twelve items off the average bride's sixteen-month planning checklist to get everything done. Kim and Bradley decided early to have a lot of do-it-yourself elements to their wedding and they wanted to be as earth-friendly as possible. After all, it was Kim's love of the outdoors and tomboyish childhood that led her to live and breathe a little game of balls and strikes – a child's game she had the privilege of playing still as an adult. The couple's wedding invitations resembled the tickets sold at Wrigley Field; their centerpieces were vases filled with baseballs. Throughout the history of weddings, many couples have chosen to incorporate a baseball theme. But no baseball wedding seemed as special as the one where Kim Reedeaux, the Cubs' first female baseball star, was the bride.

To honor the minute that most afternoon Cub home games would begin at Wrigley during baseball season, Kim Reedeaux – at exactly 1:20 p.m. Central Time on January 22, 2010 – was escorted down the aisle by her father and soon thereafter she became Mrs. Bradley James. The newlyweds' reception consisted of ballpark food, a first dance to "Take Me Out to the Ballgame," and an atmosphere as electric as if the Cubs had just won the World Series. Kim was so happy that she felt like she had won the World Championship. Yet, in the back of her mind, a cynic developed and she wondered if her team would ever win again. She was happy to have survived a year of injuries, a stalker, and wedding planning to remain a baseball player at the Big League level, but as hard as she wanted to ignore her gut, she began to doubt her Cubbies' ability to win.

Pitchers and catchers reported to Mesa for the start of 2010 Spring Training on February 17. Fans were excited for that day, a good month before it came, posting poems like *Roses are red, Violets are short, in a few short days, pitchers and catchers report!* Just a few short days – and a quick honeymoon – after the team's battery mates arrived, Kim began preparations for her personal comeback year and first season as a married woman.

Instead of being met with fanfare and happiness, with thousands of fans excited to see her play, Kim faced a tired crowd, well-tired by the drama, gossip, and news of her off-the-field nightmare, stories aired only after an injury-plagued season. Stereotypical as it may seem, a male player succumbs to injuries all season and the fan will chalk it up as "the injury bug" or "he'll come back stronger next year." Let the girl face an injury – or worse yet – harassment, and suddenly she is eyed as a liability, too emotional, and unworthy of a fan's unrelenting support. The cheers, standing ovations, and excitement from the fans that came out to support the team waned every time Kim stepped up to the plate. That excitement now appeared for the next phenom, new Cubs shortstop Toby Akihito. Akihito, a twenty-six-year-old success story from the Japanese league came to the Cubs in an off-season bid and brought with him tremendous promise for the future and one goal in mind: to win the starting spot at short. Akihito's success meant battling Kim for the spot and he was just young, brave, and talented enough to not care about the hype or hoopla of the "girl." No one could blame him; it is every player's dream to start in the Big Leagues. Kim had lived that dream herself. By all accounts, Kim was yesterday's news to the fans, the sportswriters, the broadcasters, and in some degree, to her teammates. She had her moment; her moment faded. She knew it. Akihito was the future of the franchise, so Kim – in a move still praised – made a totally selfless decision to let the rookie live his dream.

On February 27, 2010, just thirty-six days after she said "I do" and a few short days before the Cubs' first Spring Training game, Kim decided to put marriage before the Majors and again walk away from the game she loved. She could have never predicted "what might have been" or if Akihito would have made the team over her, regardless, but her departure ensured the kid would get the chance to prove himself. Kim was all about helping the next generation – in all walks of life, not just baseball.

When the Cubs' spring campaign ended – if anyone cared as dismal as it was – the team was 4½ games out of first place in Cactus League play with a record of 8–12 and just that quickly, no one mentioned Kim Reedeaux at all. Star rookie Akihito pulled his left hamstring in the third preseason game, missed the rest of the spring and never made it back to the Majors all season. The Cubs traded for a center fielder from the Brewers in July, just before the deadline, and picked up a shortstop from the A's in a three team "fire-sale" deal with the Royals.

As Kim watched the evening news one night and heard that the Cubs notched another loss, Kim asked only one question: "Did it ever matter?"

"Did what matter?" Brad asked, as he put his arms around her, cuddled on the couch.

"Me. Baseball. Any of it?" Kim asked, acting somewhat dejected.

"You doubt it?" Brad said, giving Kim a look.

"You don't?"

Brad didn't say a word. His stern, serious, "oh please" look said enough, even if Kim was not convinced.

Whether Kim's absence was to blame or if the team simply struggled that much was hard to say, but the Cubs less-than-par Spring Training, little as the season preview generally means, was largely accurate for how the season would go. By the time Wayne Messmer had sung the National Anthem and the last guest conductor of the seventh inning stretch had belted out something resembling "Take Me Out to the Ballgame" for the final time in the 2010 season, the Cubs had finished 75–87 for the season, their only winning month coming in September when the pressure was gone. With just a 44% winning percentage at the Friendly Confines at Wrigley, the fans – like Kim – began to question if the team really wanted to win.

Faith may have fled from many Cub fans, but the biggest fan of one former female MLB shortstop believed in his wife. He had faith in Kim, even when she had no faith in herself and he refused to believe that 2010 was the end of Kim Reedeaux, as she was still known professionally, and the little game of balls and strikes she loved so much. The game and Kim were as married as Bradley and she.

Ultimately, Bradley's belief in Kim later became the driving force behind one upcoming at-bat in the ninth inning of Game 7 in the World Series with Kim at the plate, ready for a date with destiny.

CHAPTER 23

Over the course of sports history, many players have retired, only to return to the sport – a brief time later – to have successful "comebacks" in the sports they loved. Throughout sports from Michael Jordan to Pelé to Brett Favre to the Pittsburgh Penguins' Mario Lemieux, sports stars' comeback stories were widely hailed as successful. In baseball, there have been several such stories.

In 1922 and 1923, Paul Schreiber pitched a few games for the Brooklyn Robins before spending the next decade in the Minor Leagues. He retired to become a coach in 1931. In 1945, the Yankees – and their war-depleted lineup – offered Schreiber, then forty-two years old, the opportunity to return to the Majors. He pitched two games in 1942 and his twenty-two-year gap between Major League seasons will likely never be broken.

In late October of 2013, three full years and incredibly bleak seasons of Cubs baseball from the fan's point of view later, Kim Reedeaux decided that the daily grind of a housewife was no longer her cup of tea. She longed to be a Cub again; she longed to prove herself again; she longed to smell the grass from field level again; she longed to live her life again. Her life was baseball and it had been for over forty years. Could a forty-one-year-old shortstop, three years removed from the game, the sounds, the signals, the calls, and all things baseball ever find her form again? Surely, if Paul Schreiber could do it in the 1940s, Kim Reedeaux could in the twenty-first century.

For the last three seasons, other than being a fan who watched the game from the stands or on television, Kim had scrubbed the floors, washed the cars, cooked the family dinners, and played with her three "children" – bulldogs Santo, Brickhouse, and Caray – named after three of the most beloved Cub broadcasters to ever grace the air.

The game still ran through her veins and every time she watched a game, read a column, took a caller during fill-in radio shifts, or petted her dogs, Kim's love for the game beat as strongly as her heart.

The top four components that any baseball player needs in a conditioning regimen are mental, strength, speed, and agility workouts. If completed in combination, these four workouts can, in theory, bring any baseball player committed to a comeback back from the graveyard of ball players past. Since her resignation, retirement, extended vacation, or lengthy "honeymoon phase" – call it whatever you wish – Kim had, in her own way, kept herself in decent shape. After all, had she ever really intended to walk away from the game forever? No. As most big-hearted individuals who play for the love of the game, not the luxuries or money it provides – rare as those players are in today's era – Kim sincerely walked away to give Akihito a chance. That she questioned if her career had mattered and questioned the Cubs' ability to win was purely self-deprecation and the mindset of the fan on many days. Every Cub fan, at one point or another, has asked if the Cubs are capable of winning. You could read it on message boards, see it in the looks on the faces of dejected fans after a loss, hear it in the voices of the fans when they'd boo or call local sports radio shows, and taste it in the bitterness of every October when other teams found postseason/World Series glory while the Cubs sat sidelined.

The Cubs' Akihito experiment turned out to be a dud. After three seasons, Cubs dealt the young, injury-prone Akihito to the White Sox for a future prospect and cash. The Wrigleyville fans, totally loyal to Cub Nation, saw the trade as dumping their "trash" in the "baddest part of town," to quote the late Jim Croce. The White Sox fans saw the move as a positive and took shots at the Cubs, yet again, calling them "that little North Side Farm Club." The Akihito experience and the Cubs' time invested into it embodied the same philosophy as other players the team babied past their prime. All teams do, really. A team bills a player up to be the next big superstar and one of two things happen: either the player's head swells to the size of a watermelon, causing their self-worth to become more inflated than a helium balloon that pops against a vaulted ceiling or the player works so hard to fulfill the overblown expectations the team has laid out for him that either the player – or his coaching staff – overwork him, exhaust him, or indirectly injure him by forcing him to work so hard. Sadly, the latter scenario happens far too often. Great prospects can have their careers ended, and they find life on their own. But, that's baseball and the baseball life – a life that Kim Reedeaux loved.

In November 2013, Kim, her husband, and the dogs loaded the Jeep and headed for Arizona. Steak and sodas gave way to salads and weight-loss shakes just to ensure Kim would return to tip-top form by Spring Training 2014. First, however, she needed an invitation. Kim simply wanted an opportunity. Every big comeback story needs a starting point. Kim Reedeaux-James jumped up and down on Valentine's Day Eve 2014, having secured a non-roster invitee invitation to Cubs' Spring Training. With that invitation, she found her starting point. What she did not realize is that her very own "Field of Dreams" was just beginning.

Cub fans were unsure how to react to Kim's Spring Training appearance. She was there, gone, back, gone and now back again after a three-year break. To some, the forty-one-year-old seemed like baseball's version of Brett Favre, the ex–Green Bay Packer so long unable to walk away from his love for the game and accept what God had willed to be. While some hedge at incorporating God in baseball, Kim believed that her life held a higher purpose. She believed she had survived the challenges, taken her lumps, and fought back stronger than ever for reasons greater than her own will. Sure, there were times when, in human nature, she doubted her faith but in those times, her husband or the memory of Anna Merkel were always there to remind her.

Kim began Spring Training with a new outlook and new ritual. Before each game, Kim would pull Anna's note from her locker, hold it to her eyes, and give it a butterfly kiss. Then, she would blow on the paper to send the kiss on its way and say a small prayer that each game would bring her one step closer to her ultimate dream of making the team and getting the Cubs back to the postseason and beyond.

As a player and a fan, Kim looked forward to the day when the Cubs would go far beyond the regular season, reaching a place much higher, more beautiful and overflowing with grandeur than Cub fans had known in over 100 years; a place where mortals hail, angels praise and dreams encompass all who are fortunate enough to grace the halls; where all MLB World Champions reside in their own special corner of what can only be described as baseball heaven; where each World Series victor's success is preserved for all eternity and where the same reflections would find Heaven on Earth in Cooperstown. Yes, indeed, that's where Kim wanted to be. That's where Anna's every dream would come true. That's where the dream of every Cub fan to have lived, loved, breathed, and died with their team for over a century would finally find its wings.

The thought of being in the World Series and in the position of being the one to make-or-break the long-standing curse excited Kim, but of course, she needed to ensure her spot on the team, then play the season – a season in which the Cubs were projected to do nothing and go nowhere under new management and with young players – and go from there.

Kim's new outlook became apparent in her first Spring Training game. Toned, ready, and excited, Kim walked onto the field with Journey's "Don't Stop Believin'" blaring in the background. The music could not have been more fitting for the game, the spring, and the season about to unfold. She was healthy, happy, strong, and secure. The only thing she longed for was baseball and a season of baseball is what she would have.

In her first five games, Kim hit .364 with a double, a triple, and two homers – the Cubs' only two runs in a 9–2 loss to the Diamondbacks. In those twenty-two at-bats, Kim only struck out twice. She out-fielded, out-hit, and out-hustled her teammates; she outsmarted the competition. Suddenly, the only criticism the sportswriters could find was that maybe Kim was trying too hard, would run out of steam, and would alienate her teammates by making them all look bad. She was determined – and some could say destined – to make this team and sure enough, when camp broke for Opening Day in Chicago, Kim was there, ready, willing and able to do whatever it took to avoid sabotage, stalkers, curses, and critics to play the kind of baseball she wanted – the winning kind. It would not take long for Kim's incredibly positive attitude to infect the entire team.

Opening Day at Wrigley Field came on Monday, April 7, 2014, and there was something more magical in the air than the typical Opening Day at Wrigley. The season began sixteen days shy of the historic ballpark's 100th anniversary. Despite four straight lackluster, less than stellar seasons, each filled with some form of drama on and off the field, the Cubs with the no-name manager and no-name players, to hear the sportswriters' vantage points, were largely under no expectations and no pressure. The fans debated what to make of Kim's return – was it beneficial to the team or not; they were equally split over how pathetic this team might be. A few fans even paraphrased lines from the movie *Major League* while questioning who the coaches, players, and staffers were. If one word could best describe the Cubs' "No Name" 2014 roster, that word was fearless. When Kim's spring campaign took off, the atmosphere changed. Suddenly, she went from the publicity stunt or diva, as some previously viewed her, to the forty-one-year-old veteran on a team where the average Opening Day starting age was twenty-six years and eight months. Her younger teammates followed her example and their own Spring Training outings benefited. The Cubs, usually prey to lousy March outings, achieved a winning Spring Training record for the first time in years.

When interviewed by WGN-TV, during the *Lead-Off Man* broadcast on Opening Day, Kim said she felt like a big sister to her teammates. She laughed when the play-by-play guy said, "Or the mother that returned to college to get her degree after raising her own kids." Kim, quick to respond through her laughter, said, "Yes, my degree would be a World Championship for the Cubs." Kim Reedeaux, consummate professional and team player, always. She was a great player for the team, as well.

The 2014 season opened against the nearby rival Milwaukee Brewers. The weather proved to be typical for Chicago in April: uncertain. As the first pitch crossed home plate, the temperature was 47 degrees; the wind blew 25 miles per hour, straight off Lake Michigan, and conditions seemed favorable for homers falling to Waveland if anyone connected with the ball. Surprisingly, the first three innings were quiet. The Brewers' fourth inning was as well. There was tension as two veteran pitchers battled each other to see which team's offense could crush the other's defense first. The bottom of the fourth saw Cubs' third baseman Joel Kellogg on first; it was time for Kim's second at-bat of the game. On an 0–2 count – her pressure-loving favorite of all counts – Kim launched an 87 mph fastball into the left field bleachers to put the Cubs ahead, 2–0. They would not trail again in the game. As "Go Cubs Go" blared for the 41,000 chilly fans, a new age of Cubs baseball was just beginning. Cub fans hadn't seen anything yet!

CHAPTER 24

The All-Star Game is a time of much fanfare and merriment for everyone in Major League Baseball and its fans. For the fans, the game provides a chance to enjoy the memories of younger days, to vote for their favorite players in hopes of helping them make the team, and to experience the beauty in the host city or ballpark. For Major League Baseball's thirty teams, there is much more at stake: the chance for home-field advantage in the World Series.

For the Chicago Cubs, the World Series may have seemed like a pipe dream. After all, their last appearance in a World Series game was in 1945, nearly seventy years ago; their last World Series victory was in 1908, 106 years ago. To say that time was running out for the great-great-great-grandparents of society, getting by day by day in America's nursing homes, to witness what they'd likely only seen as newborns – a Cubs' World Series victory – was an understatement. After all, those alive to have witnessed the last Cub appearance in the World Series were well past retirement age and enjoying the game with their grandchildren now. Cub fans are resilient, but resilience can only take a person so far. The All-Star Break in 2014 displayed the Cubs' best first half of the season in many years and saw a baseball first: Kim Reedeaux made the National League All-Star roster. The Cubs were first in the N.L. Central with the best winning percentage in the entire National League. Hopes were high, but Cub hopes were often high, only to be dashed by heartbreak later. Cub fans, like the team, knew to take each game, one at-bat at a time. Any additional hope beyond that and heartache could easily ensue.

The setting for the 2014 All-Star Game was Target Field in Minneapolis, the newest home of the Minnesota Twins. Nearly forty years earlier, Harold Reedeaux had moved his family from the Gopher State. Now, in this homecoming, he would have the opportunity to see his daughter shine as a member of the National League All-Stars, representing his Chicago Cubs. Harold Reedeaux was a very proud father.

Several thousand journalists traveled to Minneapolis to cover the All-Star Game and nearly all of them vied for an interview with the sport's #1 "go-to girl." The media darling she was, as a player and a sports jock, Kim talked with every interviewer she could, always gracious and appreciative for the opportunity God gave her. She had enjoyed a remarkably solid first half of the 2014 season. By the middle of May, as fan voting for the All-Star Game ramped up, Kim had notched thirteen home runs – to lead the Majors. She also led the League in on-base percentage, batting, extra-base hits, doubles and total bases. Those that followed the prior stages in Kim Reedeaux's career knew that Spring Training was special; by the All-Star Break, every baseball fan in the country and world knew Kim Reedeaux was special. Through her childhood, girls everywhere had longed to have her naturally long eyelashes; now, girls everywhere aspired to be Kim when they grew up.

Each year, the Home Run Derby features eight players and Kim was excited to show the "boys" what she had, as one of the selected few. She looked to make her family, her fans, her team, her hometown, and her city proud.

Rare, stifling heat welcomed players and fans to Minnesota for that Monday night. Very little breeze blew and some media personnel wondered how the stillness would impact the home run counts that night. Local meteorologists noted how the unseasonably hot temperatures made this Home Run Derby the hottest in the event's nearly thirty-year history. Kim was the first up to swing for her life that night. After all, the Golden Rule of life is ladies first. At the plate, Kim smiled, trying to take in the fun of the moment, but it wasn't just about the fun – it was about making an impact: her impact, not just with the ball, but also in the sport itself. The first two pitches she faced were outs. She paused for a third. She barely launched the fourth pitch into home run territory, but then she went on a tear. Pitch after pitch went sailing into the summertime skies over Downtown Minneapolis and the fans could not get enough of it.

By the end of round one, Kim was in second place with eight homers; one home run behind Prince Fielder. She easily advanced as one of four players to square off in round two. Whispered chatter from some of the first round's send-offs implied that Kim, as a female, would not have the power, or the arm, to hold up for another round in the

Home Run Derby. Kim, with her jackrabbit-like ears, overheard the rumblings and was more inspired to prove the critics wrong. So what did Kim do in the second round of the Home Run Derby? She led the final four participants with an additional twelve home runs, one run more than Prince Fielder.

After her showing in round two, Kim walked over to her critics and said, "What did you all think of that?" Kim Reedeaux: never one to take crap from anyone. Her father and a long-time mentor had both told her that at a much younger time in her life; their advice was the best that any two people could have given.

The final round of the Home Run Derby pitted Fielder against Reedeaux; the son of an ex-Major Leaguer against the daughter of a retired sports radio legend; guy versus girl and two ex-division rivals squaring off for destiny. And Destiny is a girl's name. This time Destiny called Kim's name. When batting in the final round was completed, records fell like raindrops on the ivy walls of the Friendly Confines. Those records belonged to Kim Reedeaux. The rock star shortstop for the Cubs hit thirteen home runs to Prince Fielder's twelve in the final round, slamming the thirteenth and winning homer with only six of her ten allotted outs recorded. Her baker's dozen homers broke the final round record and the next day, all the sportswriters could say is maybe "Next Year Is Now" for the Cubs because their publicity stunt is actually talented. Kim, who never liked reading the sports section on game days or when big series – like Cubs vs. Cardinals – arrived, could not help but read the feedback for her Home Run Derby performance. She sat, she read, she laughed, she smiled, and she laughed again when local radio played "My Way" and referenced her afterwards. Kim had always done things her own way and her way often proved to be the right way!

That night, that magical night beneath the moonlight of Minnesota's "City of Lakes," Kim Reedeaux found herself at the plate with the bases loaded and two out in the ninth inning of a tied game. If she laid down a hit, the National League would have home field advantage in the World Series and Kim was convinced the Cubs would be there. She was a dreamer, like every Cub fan, but she carried that much faith in her team, too. Then, the unthinkable happened. Boston Red Sox pitcher, Leon Chapman, many times over All-Star and extreme jerk in the eyes of women everywhere; the man who had refused to sign Kim's baseball, years ago; the man who corked her bat and ended her first stint in the Majors; the man most hated by everyone in Kim's family, close or extended, was brought in to pitch.

I can only assume that the American League manager felt that this would throw Kim off her game. It didn't. In fact, Leon's history with Kim and his overbearing ego only served to prove Kim's point when it came to him. Kim Reedeaux, married and forty-two years old, played the game because she loved it; she loved the fans, she loved the sights, smells, and fresh air. Leon Chapman, woman hater and forty-six-year-old, played the game because he had nothing else in his life if he stopped. Kim played for the love of the game; Leon, the love of the money.

Any Major Leaguer looking to settle an old score with another player in the situation Kim faced could easily choose to knock the ball out of the park, live up the Grand Slam, and laugh as he touched each base to rub it in the face of the despised one. This was not Kim's nature. Kim's nature was the calm approach, the mental approach: hit the evil one in a way that is clever, crafty, not blatantly obvious but obvious enough that the nemesis and you will always know what happened.

On a 3–2 count with two outs and the bases loaded in the bottom of the ninth inning, Kim Reedeaux patiently drew a walk. It was a free pass that put her on base, walked in a run, and won the All-Star Game for the National League. More importantly, Kim ensured home field advantage for the World Series.

As Kim walked away from the hugs and high fives of her fellow National League All-Star teammates, Leon Chapman approached her with one message: "Pull that stunt again and you'll never play in this League again." Kim simply nodded, smiled, and went to find her dad. Just a few months later, as the Red Sox and Cubs returned to the field after a lengthy rain delay in Game 7 of the World Series with two on, two out and Kim Reedeaux at the plate in the bottom of the ninth, Leon Chapman readied for revenge on the hallowed ground where his career began. He longed to be the ultimate Cubs' dream crusher, because that's just the kind of person Leon Chapman always was.

CHAPTER 25

In 2012, Major League Baseball announced its first postseason playoff change since 1995. The change involved implementing a new playoff format where each league added a second wildcard qualifier, creating a ten-team playoff format. The two wildcard qualifiers from each league would have a one-game playoff to determine which team advances to the Division Series to play the division champion with the best overall regular season record.

With so many teams during the 2011 season vying for postseason glory with just days to go in the season, fans across Major League Baseball were excited to welcome this new format change. This decision still left Cub fans optimistic, though it had not improved their team's 2012 and 2013 outcomes.

So many times of the course of the Cubs' last 106 years, the team appeared destined to reach the playoffs, only to falter in the season's last few weeks or days. In the few times the team did make the playoffs, Bartman balls, goat curses, and black cats seemed to blindside fate. Fate often catches the blame, but in reality, what the Cubs experienced for many years was a lack of faith. The countless years when sportswriters and even some fans dubbed the team the "Loveable Losers," "The Cellar Dwellers," "That Northside Farm Club," created an atmosphere of cloudy skies and dampened spirits. The negative connotations caused players to only give fifty percent about twenty percent of the time, some years. The 2014 season brought with it the Lake Michigan–kissed winds of change, because of one star shortstop.

The Cubs' momentum continued on the upswing after the All-Star Break. They split a series with the Reds followed by winning back-to-back series against the Pirates and the Mets. The club finished the month of July with a four-game winning streak after taking care of the Padres at Wrigley. They were six games over .500 and still maintaining the lead in the Central by 2½ games. Kim, the timeless shortstop that could, cheered every win as proudly as the Wrigleyville fans. She was having the time of her life.

August ushered in a difficult schedule and every Cub player and fan knew the month could make or break the team. The Brewers were beginning to find their power and their power seemed to fly out of the park on angel wings. By the 12th of August, the Cubs' season-long momentum of steel began to crumble amid summertime heat-related illness and exhaustion. The media began to speculate that the team had peaked too soon. Kim Reedeaux, of course, refused to hear it. Sick one August series, thanks to some bad crab meat served in Miami, Kim still kept a positive attitude. Her faith in her team, their ability to win, and herself was so strong that she suggested that others might want to join her in praying for the team's healing.

"I refuse to pray this personally," Kim explained, "but if anyone wants to also pray that we hang on and make the postseason, go ahead." Her teammates started to complain.

"You don't pray for us to win?" first baseball Eric Belmont asked.

"No, I don't. I pray for our ability and our strength. God grants our ability; we have to produce or the ability is lost," Kim sternly announced.

"So you don't believe God makes us win?" inquired center fielder Raul Perez.

"We make us win. Our faith in ourselves makes us win. Our faith in Him makes Him proud. He, in turn, rewards us by giving us the abilities we have to get the job done."

Everyone may have their own interpretations of what makes a baseball player a winner. What leads them to connect with the ball, run faster than the opponent to safely slide into third or to knock an 88-mph fastball over 500 feet? For Kim, talent – God-given talent – was only as good as the belief of those blessed with it. Use a God-given talent incorrectly or abuse its worth and a person's pursuit fails; use it wisely, for the purpose of good, and success comes with it. What was the Cubs' purpose of good? To the team – and to especially Kim – it was helping the fans, the City, the State of Illinois, the country and of course, themselves to achieve something so long-awaited and dubbed improbable that a Cubs World Series victory was spoofed in a video game, just two years before.

After Kim's speech about faith refocused the team, they never looked back again. Despite injuries, illnesses and a tough August schedule, a six-game winning streak helped the Cubs finish the month of August better than they had entered it. As they stared the month of September, the last month of the season, in the face, Kim and her teammates joined in one circle and prayed for health, happiness, and homers in the month of September. Yes, even Kim went back on her word and prayed for homers. Hits, home runs – to Kim it didn't matter. Her dream had become the team's dream at last; the farm team references were long gone and even a few White Sox fans, diehard to the South Side haven, could not be happier for what was shaping up to be "the year" – or at least the best shot the Cubs had known in a very long time.

On September 1st, the Cubs were in St. Louis and dropped what Chicago sports radio announcers jokingly called a "heartbreaker" 8–1. The lone run was a solo shot by Kim, her first homer in six weeks and twentieth of the season. A Chicago-based Cardinals fan called WGN radio and said "That Kim Reedeaux is setting records right and left – oh wait, she's a girl. Go figure." For the next hour, the WGN studio lines lit up with Cub fans wanting to discuss nothing but that caller. Radio caller and radio caller trashed the devout – and some would say dumb – Cardinal fan. The fans called the poor hopeless sap every name in the book and one fan – whose prediction is still discussed today – said "Hey, Mr. Smarty Pants, may we meet you in the Division Series and may we kick your…" Before the last word sprang from his mouth, the call abruptly ended; we can all assume what the loyal Cub fan meant. I heard the caller; I sensed his frustration and loyalty to the Cubs. I admired his passion for Kim's abilities and yes, I echoed his sentiment, under my breath. Every Cub fan across the country did. To the opposing team's announcers, the opposing city's sportswriters, and maybe some of the other team's diehard fans, Kim Reedeaux was still a vixen, a publicity stunt, and all the other names she had been called but the respect she commanded and earned was just that – commanded and earned. She paid her dues and then some; she was on a winning Chicago Cubs team because she helped them to win.

After the Cardinal fan nearly incited a riot among Cubs fans from Hawaii to Maine and Texas to Minnesota, the Cubs went on a five-game winning streak. Kim was flawless – she hit, she walked, she doubled, she tripled, she practically stood on her head to catch fly outs and she turned three beautiful 6-4-3 double plays in one game, all with her dyed brown ponytail pulled through her baseball cap. No one could say she was a forty-two-year-old past her prime. She proved every day that life begins at forty.

The Cubs, securely in the playoffs without much question, slacked a little and dropped five straight after the five-game winning streak. On 9/11, the fifth anniversary of the day when a stalker forced Kim away from the sport and her husband later proposed marriage; the Cubs won a 3–2 matchup with the Phillies and extended their season record to 86 wins and 62 losses. At the start of the season, no one saw this franchise – a team that left people questioning who the players were and a coaching staff as unknown as those that took to the hallowed ground of Wrigley – as a winner. Now, everyone did.

Journey's "Don't Stop Believin'" became the team's September anthem and on the old Lowrey organ, it sounded really sweet. The anthem became as popular as "Take Me Out to the Ballgame" or "Go Cubs Go," which – go figure – fans sang often in the 2014 season. If any fan didn't know the words to any of those songs before the month of September that year, they knew them by the 30th.

Cubs' management asked Wayne Messmer, the Voice of the Cubs – often dubbed "the guy that sings the Anthem" – to surprise the fans on the last home game of the season by belting out "Don't Stop Believin'" along with the National Anthem and "God Bless America." He gladly accepted. To Cubs Nation, Wayne Messmer could have become the new Steve Perry; there wasn't a quiet mouth in the house, as everyone sang along and the cheers rang for five minutes before the final home game began. The excitement within the hallowed walls of Wrigley Field had never been greater and through all the years of heartbreak, Cub fans did not believe heartbreak was anywhere in the Midwest, let alone Illinois or more specifically, Wrigleyville. When the final regular season game came to a close and the Cubs had knocked off Kim's hometown Pittsburgh Pirates one last time for the 2014 season, the team and the fans celebrated for more than an hour. The Cubs final regular season record: 96–66; thirty games over .500, the National League Central Division Champions.

Under the new playoff format, the Cubs with the best division record in the National League, secured the top seed in the playoffs and would play the winner of the Cardinals-Dodgers playoff game. Confident they could beat either of those teams, the Cubs – especially Kim – and even more especially, their fans, hoped and prayed the Cardinals would win, just so everyone could pray for revenge against that inconsiderate Cardinal fan. One bad fan can spoil an entire team and city's view on an organization, but of course, there had never been much love lost between the Cards and Cubs.

On Friday, October 3rd, Cub fans everywhere watched as the St. Louis Cardinals fell to the Dodgers 7–5 in 11 innings. The only thing nearly every Cub fan said was "Serves that fan right"; the only thing the Cubs team said, "Let's get ready for the Dodgers."

Opening night of the NLDS was a cold night even for Chicago standards in early October. The north wind off Lake Michigan, kicked up by a passing early fall cold front, whipped at 25 mph with gusts approaching 40 at times. Regardless of the cold conditions, the standing-room-only crowd embraced the star-filled night in the heavens and on the field. The stands, bleachers, and luxury boxes featured many stars themselves. Celebrities flocked to Chicago to see their LA Dodgers; those stars with ties to Chicago proudly arrived in Cubs gear and mingled with their fellow Bleacher Bums. The beautiful ivy covering the outfield wall began its annual change and displayed a hint of brown. For the Cubs faithful, hopes rang eternal that the beloved team that frolicked within the shell of the 100-year old Friendly Confines would not morph into their winter form anytime soon.

Cub fans would rock Wrigley for the first two games of the NLDS and rock Wrigley they did, so much that the players' bats started rocking too. By the fourth inning of Game 1, the Cubs were up 8–2. Each time Kim Reedeaux came to the plate, you would have thought the fans were living the good old days of ZZ Top or Aerosmith concerts. It was hard for anyone to hear themselves think; hearing anyone speak was next to impossible. By seventh inning stretch time, with the Cubs up 9–4, Rick Springfield – who launched his own comeback tour earlier in 2014 – could have sung "Auld Lang Syne" and no one would have known any differently. Cub fans would have still sung "Take Me Out to the Ballgame" and prayed that Hall-of-Famer Ron Santo was sitting on a cloud willing his team to victory. Every Cub fan believed again; every Cub player believed again. It was indeed a beautiful thing.

The Cubs won Game 1 by the final score of 10–5. They won Game 2 in eleven innings after Kim drove in the winning run on a double that kissed the Center Field wall. Up two games to none and headed to Los Angeles, the Cubs knew no cockiness. They'd been in this position before and tragedy, drama, or curses took the beautiful possibilities that could be in the National League Championship Series and threw it away like an empty hot dog wrapper.

Game 3 in Los Angeles became a little game later known as "The Kim Reedeaux Show." No, this was not a play on her other career as a sports radio goddess; game 3 was Kim's night to shine. She wanted to put her team into the NLCS for the first time since 2003 and the Bartman Ball incident. Craig Credan, Kim's college friend and devoted Cub fan who had sat one row ahead of Steve Bartman, the over-exuberant Cub fan who interfered with the ball eleven years earlier and cost the Cubs their last opportunity to reach the NLCS, flew to Los Angeles for the game. Craig and Kim had maintained their friendship over the course of twenty years and he was eager to support her and his beloved Cubs. No one knew if Kim's awesome night was due to her friend's attendance, her long-standing goal to go the distance for her team, or because she wanted to impress her dad, but whatever the reason, she hit for the cycle – including a three-run homer – and helped her team sweep the Dodgers in the National League Division Title. One step down, two steps to go for World Series greatness. The next stop: the NLCS with the New York Mets.

The New York Mets forged quite the history both with the Cubs and with Kim. The Cubs had suffered heartbreak at the hands of the Mets before, though it had been roughly forty-five years. Harold Reedeaux flew into Chicago, eager to witness a Cubs-Mets game at Wrigley, unlike what he was able to do in 1976. Realistically, he was more eager to support Kim and her dream. Proud fathers everywhere could dispute Harold's chokehold on "proudest father in the world" but his heart swelled with pride for his baby girl. The special bond between Kim and Harold always painted the perfect picture of family and love. At the age of seventy-six, Harold could think of no place in the world he'd rather be.

The 45th NLCS began October 15th at Wrigley Field before a crowd of 43,000 eager fans. Fans everywhere predicted how many games the series would go – five was the most popular guess – and many of those fans also predicted the results. Loyal Chicago-based Cub fans, of course, sided with their ball club; the rest of Cub Nation? Not so much. Sure every Cub fan everywhere wanted to see the team in the World Series, but the odds and history were certainly not in their favor. Speaking of odds, the betting public in Las Vegas put the Cubs' chances of reaching the World Series at 5–1. It became quite clear to the team that their most loyal fans were true blue always; the rest were fair-weather, to some degree. Kim Reedeaux would never bet against her team, not only because the practice is illegal but because her faith was too strong. The queen of the comeback, the dreamer and the MVP of the NLDS, Kim loved high odds. She had stood before high odds many times over her twenty-plus-year pursuit of baseball greatness. She faced every sky-high odds board in the face and depressed everyone that had bet against her success. She even told a reporter in an interview once, "I live for sky-high odds; the higher the odds, the better my success rate." Many people laughed when she said that, but the former preemie meant business. She meant business on the field that October 15th night also.

The first pitch of the Cubs first NLCS in ten years crossed home plate for a ball at 3:05 p.m. Central Time on October 15, 2014. Any fan that enjoyed an exciting back-and-forth affair would be in for a treat. The Mets manufactured a run in the first on a leadoff walk, followed by two singles, one with two outs in the inning. The Cubs answered in the bottom of the first with a two-run homer off the bat of Derek Lopez, the Cubs' power-hitting second baseman. Baseball's latest edition of an epic ESPN Classic–worthy duel began. The score remained unchanged for three more innings. In the top of the fourth, the Mets stamped a three-run homer and air mailed it to Waveland Avenue for the overflowing crowds outside the stadium to die a little. The Mets added a fifth run in the top of the fifth. They would add just one more run in the game.

In the bottom of the fifth, Kim came to the plate to begin a Cub storm. Kim hit a single to lead off the Cubs' fifth inning. That single was followed by Gary Austere's double and Benny Alvaro's ground rule double, and then a string of hits that brought the score to 8–5 Cubs. Wrigley erupted with cheers that fans on the South Side of Chicago likely heard. Both teams would add a run apiece in the seventh and the Cubs held the lead all the way to the finish, winning Game 1 of the NLCS, 9–6. They finished the game with nine runs on eleven hits in a game that for Cub faithful was 3 hours and 35 minutes of Heaven. Their tour in Heaven was only beginning.

In Game 2 at Wrigley, the run explosion from the prior game's fifth inning largely continued. The Cubs scored twelve runs on seventeen hits, putting it away 12–3, Benny Alvaro leading the team with three doubles, three runs, a homer and five RBIs. As a total surprise to the Mets and all of Major League Baseball, the Cubs were up 2–0 on the Mets, with the Series heading back to New York.

The two teams split the first two games in New York, heading into a pivotal Game 5 at Citi Field. The scene was set. The Cubs led the NLCS by a 3–1 count. They were one win from the improbable, if not impossible, if you'd believed the sportswriters and fans on Opening Day. Chicago media, for fun, posed a question on their varied social media outlets, asking any and all happy Cub fans one question: "Would you prefer the Cubs bring it home in New York or would you prefer the Mets win this Game 5, so the Cubs will be back to Wrigley?" By an overwhelming majority – over 99% – the fans said, "Get us into the World Series in New York." It was the largest social media discussion in the history of Chicago's sports broadcasting outlets.

Game 5 of the NLCS consisted of many on-field mishaps. Luckily for the Cubs and unlike their history, the Mets committed those errors. The Cubs did not miss the opportunity to capitalize on each of them. With three runs in the second on the Mets' first error, another run in the fourth on the second error, another in the sixth on the third error and two more runs to put the game totally out of reach in the eighth on New York's fourth error, the game was 7–1 heading into the bottom of the ninth as the Mets tried to save face. The Cubs' rock solid relief staff gave the Mets nothing. The Mets fell one by one for three outs and in the most beautiful thing I have witnessed any opposing team do, over 40,000 fans at Citi Field paid the Cubs a standing ovation for making it back to the World Series for the first time since 1945. Kim could not contain her tears any longer. When interviewed, she let them pour and felt no shame for it. There was just one thing left to do: Win it all.

CHAPTER 26

The 110th World Series in Major League history began on October 19th and pitted two of the sport's most storied franchises – the Chicago Cubs and the Boston Red Sox – against each other in the best-of-seven series for the first time since 1918. That 1918 World Series went six games with the Red Sox winning the championship four games to two. Back then, the Cubs played their home games at a four-year-old ballpark known as Wrigley Field and their loss in the 1918 Series extended their World Series losing streak to ten years. In 1918, as Americans praised the ending of World War I, no one could fathom that nearly one hundred additional years would pass without a World Series title for the Chicago's North Side and her fans. Kim Reedeaux and her team of unknowns had done the impossible all season. They threw the ball, they hit the ball, and they caught the ball well. They were in the World Series because they earned it and not just in the long-suffering payment of dues sort of earning it.

The fanfare of the Cubs' World Series return even surprised the team's beloved female shortstop. Kim knew fanfare; she had witnessed several days, weeks, and months of it through her twenty-plus years of pursuing her baseball dream. What made her gladdest was that the fanfare was for the team as a whole and not just her. Kim was a dreamer, but also a realist; she knew full well that her team reached the World Series not by her stellar season alone, but by an entire team's stellar season. Cliché as it is, there is no "I" in team.

Kim, always available for interviews anytime anyone from the media wanted to talk, went into a state of hiding as the World Series merriment began. She wanted to step back and let her teammates live it up; her bigheartedness always shone brighter than the sun light streaming into Wrigley on any given day. On the eve of World Series Game 1, Kim purposefully made herself unavailable. No one saw or heard from her until her appearance became necessary, and surprisingly, no one asked. Kim was responsible, dependable and held her own baseball dreams so close to her heart that everyone knew she could never bail on her team in a situation like this.

So where had Kim been on the eve of World Series Game 1, a day certain to be among one of her life's biggest moments? Harold and Elizabeth had flown into Chicago the night before and Kim had decided to spend that final pre–World Series game day morning with her parents, husband, and furry children. For Kim, there was no better relaxation technique. That afternoon, while her mother nursed a migraine headache at Kim's home, the rest of the Reedeaux-James family spent the day at Millennium Park, picnicking, talking, playing with the dogs, and celebrating the exciting time ahead.

Kim, always with a baseball mind, said, "Hey Dad, want to have a catch?" – a reflection back to her all-time favorite baseball movie, *Field of Dreams.* Harold, ravaged by heart disease and age, slowly arose from the park bench and weakly walked to an open, quiet area of the park to toss the ball with his daughter. He knew he was likely making a mistake by agreeing to this game of catch, but he cherished these moments with Kim. Two tosses into the game, Harold found his knees hitting the ground, struggling with breathlessness. Kim and Bradley helped Harold back to the park bench; after twenty-five minutes, he became strong enough to make it to the car.

Once the family returned to Kim and Bradley's home, Harold rested in the spare bedroom. Kim and her mother begged Harold to visit the hospital. The elder Reedeaux, stubborn ex-radio jock that he was – and he had to be stubborn to argue with some over-excitable sports fans all day – refused. Just before bedtime, Kim's mother dozed in a recliner and Kim did not have the heart to wake her. Instead, Kim knocked on the spare bedroom door with her elbow; her hands carried a tray filled with a lean ham sandwich on one slice of white bread, a package of crackers, and a Coca-Cola – her dad's usual bedtime snack order.

"Here you go, Dad," Kim said with a smile.

"Service with a smile; I would expect nothing less from you, my dear." Harold doted on his daughter.

As Kim turned to leave the room, she heard, "Kim…"

"Yes, Dad," Kim said as she paused.

"I just wanted to say that I'm proud of you and you've always been a really wonderful daughter."

Kim didn't know what to say. She just smiled, said "Goodnight," walked from the room, shut the door, and cried in her husband's arms.

Resilient as Kim was, she knew her dad was ill and she knew there was nothing she could do to stop the inevitable. She merely prayed that God would keep him well until the month of October finished, regardless of the outcome in the series. Some prayers must go unanswered.

Kim awakened early on World Series Game 1 day to hear the guest bathroom shower running and her dad looking a lot better, sitting at the dining room table and peeling an orange for breakfast. With a hug and no mention of his sweet comment the night before, Kim left home to get in some early morning exercise for the big game ahead. Her pregame World Series exercise regimen had one goal in mind – light impact to ward off any threat of injuries. Once at the ballpark, she joined her teammates in a pre-practice prayer.

"Lord give us the strength to face these challenges to come and please keep our minds sharp regardless of what might come our way," Kim began.

"And let's send these Red Sox back to Beantown," one player chimed in. Kim, in her trademark, "Let's keep it serious" look, was met by a return look of "I was." Hey, what can I say? Not everyone prays the same.

Game 1 began at 7:05 Central Time. Kim's parents decided to watch the game from home due to Harold's stomach queasiness; her mom and Bradley promised Kim they would keep an eye on Harold.

"Focus on the game, honey," Bradley said, as Kim called him one final time before the pregame festivities. "Just like you and the Cubs are a team, our family is a team too."

Kim fought back tears as she uttered "I love you."

As Kim walked to the field, she glanced to the sky and spoke to God. Under her breath, she said, "Thank you, Lord, for all the blessings in my life. Win or lose these games, I've won so much because of YOU."

Game 1 began slowly. An epic pitching duel that pegged righty against lefty began and the first three and a half innings came and went scoreless. Both ball clubs' defensive games were flawless. In the bottom of the fourth, Michael Mosby took one for the team, plunked in the arm by a pitch to lead off the inning. After Kim powered her way to a double, Kevin Girvan laid down a single to drive both runners home. The Cubs were up 2–0. Riding the momentum of "Take Me Out to the Ballgame" and the seventh inning stretch, the Cubs added a third run in the bottom of the seventh and won the opener in the Series, 3–0. Eddie

Alonzo threw a six-hit shutout that was a greater pitching display than the numbers really showed.

Despite Harold, Elizabeth, and Bradley's attendance at Wrigley, the Red Sox stole Game 2 from the Cubs, winning 2–1, thanks to an umpire's need for eyeglasses. Alfonso Rickman of the Red Sox hit a bloop single and tried to steal second. He was clearly out on the play and televised replay made that blatantly obvious to anyone who enjoyed any eyesight at all. Heck, even a blind person would have agreed with the announcers, as convincingly as they told the story. He was out. The umpire robbed the Cubs, no question. The Red Sox got lucky and the Series wasn't over yet. Boston's Fenway Park became the happy hunting ground for the battle between two of the Major League's oldest teams. If one thing had become clear to everyone that followed Cubs baseball that season, it was that anytime the team had a call go against them or faced any adversity, they came fighting back.

Kim's parents traveled to Boston and witnessed a gem as Game 3 made history. Before the four hour and nineteen minute affair on October 22nd was complete, the Red Sox and Cubs racked up twenty-four runs to break the previous World Series record, set by the Cardinals and Rangers in 2011. Albert Pujols of the Cardinals said in 2011 that the twenty-three combined runs by the St. Louis and Texas franchises was "the greatest hitting performance in World Series history." Interviewed after the 15–9 Cubs victory in Game 3 of the Cubs–Red Sox showdown, Pujols admitted he'd witnessed enormous talent displayed in a manner that appeared more spectacular than anything removed from Heaven. Pujols never planned on Kim Reedeaux playing in the Series and adding two singles, five RBIs and a double to her stat sheet. Still fighting what seemed like a stomach bug and exhaustion, Harold and Elizabeth flew back to Kim's home in Chicago, confident that the series would return to Chicago. They had faith in the team and more importantly, they had faith in their daughter.

Game 4 in Boston was largely a snooze fest to watch, especially live. Exhausted from the previous night's power-hitting, record-setting display, both teams let their fatigue show. The Cubs left some people questioning if they failed to show up after Boston won the 4–0 shutout. At two games apiece, the World Series seemed to be a draw.

Game 5, the Series' and season's last in Boston, had the Game 1 starting pitchers facing off again. For Boston, Evan Connors walked two Cubbies and both scored before the end of the first inning, thanks to an error at third. For the game, the Cubs drew eleven walks; one walk, drawn by Kim, was intentional. The Red Sox seemed a little scared by her attitude and power. Despite the walks, the Cubs left eleven players on base and had not scored again. In the top of the eighth, after several Red Sox relief mix-ups, Christophe Napolitano hit a two-run double to put the Cubs up 4–0 and that is how the final game in Boston would end. It had been nearly seventy years since the last time the Cubs reached the World Series. Now, the team boarded a plane back to Chicago, up three games to two, with two opportunities to bring that long overdue trophy home.

"Sooner rather than later, boys," Kim told her teammates on the flight back to Chicago. "Let's do this sooner rather than later." Though excited that the odds were swinging the Cubs' way and optimistic that her penultimate childhood dream was nearing reality, Kim could not deny being eager to return home to her family and most importantly, her father. Family came first, even if the Cubs were a close second.

When Kim arrived home, she found her mom sitting outside enjoying the cool late night air that blew off Lake Michigan and her dad sitting at the cherry wood dining room table, listening to a Walkman while ZZ Top music blared in the background.

"Hey, Kim!" Harold smiled. "How's this for rural Minnesota surround sound?" Harold pointed to the Walkman tuned to the same station blasting from the stereo speakers. Kim rolled her eyes and laughed.

"Rural surround sound…" Kim quipped, walking away from her father. As she shook her head, all she could think was "I worried for nothing." Still laughing as she climbed into bed, Kim found peace and prayed for God to keep her family happy and safe.

The sixth game of the 2014 World Series originally scheduled for the night of October 25th was postponed to the 26th due to the threat of storms, and the game would later prove quite worthy of the wait. For the moment, though, the extra off day gave Kim and her teammates an extra day to rest and focus on their strategy for ending the franchise's long World Series drought.

When Game 6 did finally happen, it was literally a comedy of errors. The two teams committed a total of seven errors in an eleven-inning slugfest that featured a little bit of everything: sprinkles of rain, a fight between the opposing teams' right fielders, the ejection of the Cubs' manager, a thrown water cooler, a flock of birds that swarmed into the stadium for a visit, five tie scores, twenty-eight combined hits, and an eleventh-inning Red Sox home run in an 11–10 to even the series. For the 36th time in World Series history, there would be a Game 7. The 1945 Chicago Cubs, the last Cub team to reach the World Series, saw Game 7. After the Detroit Tigers scored five runs in the first inning of that game sixty-nine years earlier, the Cubs – unable to recover – lost, 9–3. Nearly seven decades later Kim Reedeaux, whose father was born eight years before his beloved Cubs last took center stage in the World Series, could not wait to fulfill destiny. Kim was sure the Cubs would win. Kim's life and the Cubs' World Series drought had traveled similar paths. Both Kim and the team faced critics and doubters but, together, they would come out on top. Kim had faith and she could not wait for her family, especially her dad, to see this dream fulfilled.

CHAPTER 27

Every baseball player is human. Throughout time, many of America's children have looked up to baseball stars as heroes and icons. To some children, Major Leaguers fill the void of a lost parent and become the "friend" that takes them away from the stressors of life. But, life stressors and the everyday, common man's emotions affect Major League baseball stars too. After all, the game is their "job," a World Series title their "bonus" for a job well done. The rest of the time, they're just like the rest of us. Their beginnings in life are largely the same.

Kim Reedeaux knew both worlds. The prestige that came with her Major League dream provided for her family but had not changed the moral fabric that God and her parents had instilled in her soul before she first held a baseball in the early 1970s. As much as Kim loved taking a three-game series from a division rival, her family mattered most; the game was the best job that a person could ever hope to have. Nothing more, nothing less. This had always been Kim's belief, but the morning of Cubs vs. Red Sox Game 7, her priorities momentarily changed.

Tossing and turning for worrying about her dad and excitement about the night ahead, Kim awoke at 5:30 in the morning and immediately turned up the heat. Bradley had left her a message next to the coffee pot before he headed off to work that simply said, "Next Year is Today!" signed with a heart and smiley face. Her father was still asleep. She turned on her radio to the tune of "Stairway to Heaven" which made her smile, and when AM drive jock Matt Sheremet ID'd the song as a tribute to the Cubs and their pursuit of baseball heaven later that night, Kim refocused on the game again.

"Hey, Kiddo!" Harold shouted, as he walked from the guest bedroom, where Kim's mother still slept. "Anything big happening today?" Kim never tired of her dad calling her "kiddo." On that day, she stood grateful for her dad's cheery good mood.

"I wouldn't know of anything, Dad. Nothing at all," Kim said, smiling. "C'mon. Let's get some breakfast." The two grabbed their winter coats and gloves, then, headed out the door for an early morning breakfast at the Salt and Pepper Diner. The sky was a dull shade of gray and a light mist fell as the two walked towards Kim's blue Land Rover. The prospect of breakfast with her dad, while mingling with loyal Cub fans that shared her excitement for the Game 7 ahead, was moving. Kim made her love for her family evident; everyone knew her special closeness to her dad. But, the mutual love that Kim and the fans shared for the Cubs, combined with the fans' love for her, made the morning more special. Stopped at a traffic light, Kim glanced at her father. In that second, her entire baseball journey was reflected in the corner of his eye.

The moment that Kim and Harold walked through the door of the popular diner on Clark Street, the building erupted with cheers. Fans spotted Kim immediately. Unfazed by a stalker and unafraid of injury, Kim stopped to chat with every person in the restaurant that late October morning. She posed for photos with a few fans that visited from out of town and invited her dad to be in every picture. Her success began because of her parents' support. Kim never lost sight of that. She wanted her journey to be her dad's as well. Once the fanfare subsided, a young college student, waiting tables to pay tuition, brought Kim and Harold a menu.

"If you order a Bloody Mary, Ms. Reedeaux," the waiter stated, "I will not serve it. We need your head clear tonight." He tapped Kim on the shoulder and she chuckled. That was the kind of difference Kim had made to the fans and the City of Chicago. That was the difference she made to Wrigleyville.

After their Denver omelet breakfasts, Harold and Kim returned home and Kim prepared to head off to the ballpark for this much anticipated day. As she started out the door without her gloves, Harold said, "Kim. Gloves. It's cold outside." She held up her mitt and said, "Dad, this is the only glove I need."

"See you tonight, sweetheart. I love you," Harold said as Kim shut the door. Kim thought to herself, "He's seventy-six, I'm forty-two, and he's still worried I might catch a cold." Kim was not worried about catching a cold; she worried about catching every fly ball that might later come her way. As she arrived at Wrigley Field, the skies let loose and the rains poured heavier. Kim looked towards the clouds as a raindrop bounced off her nose. Reflecting back to her childhood days, she opened her mouth and let a water droplet kiss her tongue.

"Lord, I don't want a rainout tonight." This was Kim's simple prayer. She wore her game face as well as she wore her color-treated ponytail through the back of her baseball cap.

"What's with this rain?" Kim's fellow All-Star, Michael Mosby, asked.

"God's shedding his tears over our World Championship a little early." Kim said, confidently.

"Don't we have to play the game first, Kimbo?" Mike teased.

"I'm calling it, Mikey," Kim announced. "Like Babe Ruth's Called Shot, I'm calling it. We will win this game."

"Think we'll see Chapman tonight?" Mike asked, ribbing Kim.

"Depends," Kim smirked.

"Depends on?" Mike smiled, knowing where she was going with the discussion.

"Depends on if he can adjust his ahem… adult diaper." Kim laughed and it wasn't long before Mike followed suit.

Everyone knew that Leon Chapman had been around the League too long. Kim merely hoped a Cubs World Championship would prove his need to hang it up. She had one goal: Reedeaux versus Chapman, one more time. But, first, the rain needed to stop.

By the time for pregame warm-ups arrived, dark clouds hovered overhead, but the rain had slackened to an occasional sprinkle. The team took to the field for the final time in the 2014 season to stretch, practice their swings, and mentally prepare for the task at hand. The ritualistic players took to their rituals. The superstitious ones avoided black cats, ladders, and goats. Kim's pregame ritual was to chew a big wad of bubble gum and blow the largest bubble she could. If it burst quickly, she'd have a bad game; if it became large and went splat all over her face, she would have a bad fielding night; if it blew large and she had to manually pop it, her game would be a success. Like clockwork, Kim grabbed her bubble gum and began chewing. Within fifteen seconds, Kim's bubble burst. Her heart sank, but deep down, she knew she could not rely on superstition. After all, superstition wasn't what brought her to the World Series.

Kim sat in the locker room with her teammates as they prepared for the night's final showdown. She reached into her locker to grab Anna's note to give it a butterfly kiss, as she had done through her stellar Spring Training and every huge game she'd had all season. This was Kim's way of honoring the little girl that was her first "fan" in baseball and that day, her way of hopefully warding off superstitious fears. As Kim closed her eyes to "kiss" the note, the Cubs' bat boy started humming "Don't Stop Believin'." The bat boy's hum led three players to start singing and before many more seconds passed, the entire locker room was rocking to their own personal Journey cover band. Deep in Kim's soul, however, she feared the worst. What if the team was too cocky, too hyper, and too capable of blowing this? She stopped herself. Kim had taught her teammates to believe; she needed to believe. She needed to cling to her faith. As the team took the field for the pregame festivities, Kim prayed a silent prayer for her family, her team, and the fans. She prayed for their safety, their health, their happiness, and their strength. She thanked Him for her earthly gifts and those yet to unfold, because win or lose the World Series that night; she knew her life was a glorious blessing. Kim Reedeaux, the baby girl born premature who fought for survival and then for change, had witnessed glorious miracles in her forty-two years. That night, she prayed for one more.

When the pregame festivities finished, the time arrived for Kim and the Cubs to hunker down for the game of their lives. When the managers for both clubs exchanged line-up cards, the Cubs' coaching staff noticed one key change: Albert Alcala was Boston's choice to replace Red Sox Game 1 starting pitcher Patrick Houseman, who had dislocated his shoulder in warm-ups. For Kim, the matchup was silently the answer to one of her prayers. Alcala had struggled all season but the Red Sox were short-handed for fresh arms.

The game began at 7:05 Central Time and the Red Sox lead-off man singled to shallow right to start the contest. A short time later, he was picked off trying to steal second. Wrigley Field's standing-room-only crowd erupted in short-lived elation. Back-to-back doubles that sailed with the north wind that whipped into the stadium from Lake Michigan allowed two runs to score and put the Red Sox on the board with an early 2–0 lead. As quickly as Cub fans had cheered the pick-off, they turned silent over the home plate celebration and high-fives from the Red Sox teammates. After 106 years of heartbreak, the fans could not help but picture more disappointment in the offing. What fans did not realize is that the nerves and jitters of their beloved Cubs' pitcher would soon settle, those two runs would be the last the Cubs would give up in regulation, and their own display of power would not wait for long. Batting third in the Cubs' opening frame, Kim hit a line-drive deep to right center field allowing two Cubs runners to score. At the end of the first, the score was Boston 2 – Chicago 2. The score would remain there until the top of the ninth, when a home run with one aboard put the Red Sox ahead 4–2.

Dan Deerberry, manager of the Red Sox, pulled Alcala from the game after the seventh when Albert walked the bases loaded but worked his way out of it, unscathed. He turned to his equally depleted, battle-worn bullpen, where he chose twenty-seven-year-old lefty Doug Fredrickson, a rookie as green as the "Monster" at Fenway or the ivy of Wrigley in summer. Fredrickson seemed just green enough not to care about the seriousness of the situation. All greenness aside, the kid was flawless, striking out the batters in order to escape the eighth inning, tie ballgame intact. After the Red Sox were able to score in the ninth, Deerberry faced a difficult decision: keep the kid in the game for the ninth or replace him with All-Star veteran Leon Chapman for the save. With Kim certain to bat in the ninth, Deerberry chose to pull the kid for the matchup of the century – Reedeaux versus Chapman for what could be the last time in their careers.

The first two Cub batters in the ninth reached on a single and a walk; then a wild pitch allowed the runners to advance to second and third. The next two batters struck out. With two runners on, two runners out, in the bottom of the ninth, Kim headed to the plate. Before the rain delay, Leon Chapman had gone ahead in the count and had Kim down to her last strike to make the Cubs' 106-year dream come true. With the rain delay concluded, Deerberry began warming up Erich Planot to replace Chapman when Chapman tossed a cooler.

"You cannot remove me," Chapman screamed.

"It's how the game is played, Leon," Deerberry explained. "You've been around the game for over twenty years; you know how it is."

"Let me rephrase, sir," Leon said sternly. "You will NOT remove me."

"Leon, I must do what's best for the team," Manager Deerberry explained, trying not to raise his voice.

"I'm fine. Leave me in or I'll stand on the pitcher's mound and halt the game."

"You're acting like a child. Sit down."

Leon did not sit down. He walked out to the mound and began tossing a few warm-up pitches to prove his point. He looked to be in mid-season form. His anger towards Kim for her All-Star Game performance fueled every pitch he hurled. His temples tightened to expose the veins in his forehead. Against his better judgment, Deerberry decided to let Leon have his way. After all, by all rights, Chapman "should" be retiring after this game. Of course, he should have retired years ago.

Ready to resume play, Kim made a few more practice swings. She tried to put the worry of her dad's heart attack and nervous excitement about her brother Brian's attendance aside. Reedeaux and Chapman glared at each other in a battle of wills, a lengthy stare-down to see which one would blink first. As the stare-down continued, Leon knew exactly how to "handle" this woman. He had thrown three fastballs before the rain delay; he felt a curveball would speed things up and slow them enough to throw Kim off her game.

At 12:15 in the morning of October 28th, World Series Game 7 play resumed. If any fans left during the rain delay, they were definitely in the minority. Nearly everyone braved the rain, the thunder, the lightning, and the cold wind for their chance to witness a miracle on earth. Cub fans prayed Kim Reedeaux would become their patron saint. After scraping the mound, adjusting himself and twirling the ball around for the perfect setup – or stall technique – Leon was set and Kim was ready. The crowd noise was deafening and drowned out the sirens in the distance. The count resumed at one ball and two strikes.

"You're all mine, Reedeaux. The Championship is mine," Leon said as he released the pitch. Kim watched as the ball slowly came towards home plate.

"Ball!" yelled the umpire.

"Ball??!!!" Leon screamed and began to charge home plate to argue. His catcher restrained his effort.

Leon shook it off and decided to toss another curveball.

"Ball!" the umpire yelled again.

Three balls, two strikes, two on, two out. And the go-ahead run, the World Series–winning run, at the plate.

An angry Leon Chapman's face turned redder than his baseball cap.

He shook off every pitch that his catcher called until finally the catcher called time to talk with Chapman.

"Chap-stick, we can do this. Throw a slider. I have a hunch."

"I'm not throwing no daggone slider, Phil. I've been around this League nearly as long as you've been alive. Now, march your butt back to home plate and let me handle this."

Chapman's overbearing ego tied the young catcher's hands. Arguing with Chapman held no benefit. He would do what he wanted regardless. The catcher did as he was told: he left Chapman to toss his game. All Chapman accomplished was tossing the game – and the title – away. One final ball, and Kim walked to load the bases. Then Kim's fellow Chapman critic, Michael Mosby, took an 87-mph fastball deep to right center field, allowing three runs to score.

The score said it all: Cubs 5 – Red Sox 4. The Chicago Cubs were World Series Champions! As Kim and her teammates joined over 43,000 fans in singing a medley of "Go Cubs Go" and "Don't Stop Believin'," Kim blew a kiss to the sky in memory of Anna. Kim may not have been the hero that saved the day and won the World Series for the Cubs, but she held on and wore Leon Chapman down for her team. That made her a superstar.

After Kim high-fived everyone, she gave a quick glance toward the stands, hoping to see Brian; then she rushed from the postgame celebrations to be with her dad. Nothing prepared her for the hours ahead. On the way to the hospital, she called her husband to ask how Harold was doing. Brad did not answer, which left Kim fearing the worst. She called again.

"Well, Baby," Brad exhaustively continued, "the medics revived him from the first attack when we were en route to the game; later, he suffered a second. He's…"

"I should have been there; I should have been there," Kim interrupted.

"Don't do this to yourself. You know he would have wanted you to play and look what you just did. I'm so proud of you. The team, the City, everyone…we're all proud of you."

Kim's tears streamed down her face and she let them flow. All she could think about was the comment her dad made, days earlier over a ham sandwich, peanut butter crackers, and a Coca-Cola, about how proud she made her father. Did he know his health was in jeopardy? If he did, why wouldn't he let her help him? Her dad was always more important than baseball and Kim felt guilty for having focused on the game first, a morning before, as she awoke with "Stairway to Heaven."

As she pulled into the parking lot of Regional Medical Center, Kim felt lightheaded, almost as though she might collapse. The adrenaline rush of happiness combined with grief-stricken anxiety to steal what energy she had. Dizzy, she leaned against her car and called Brad to come with a wheelchair to help her inside. As the two pushed and rolled their way to the elevator, a familiar face sat in hospital lobby waiting area: Brian.

"Wait, Sweetheart," Kim said.

"What?"

"Push me over there." Kim pointed towards the man.

"Brian, is that you?" Kim asked.

"Kim, you need to get upstairs; you're delusional, you're exhausted. C'mon." Brad began pushing the wheelchair.

"Bradley Andrew James, I told you to wait," Kim shouted.

"Brian, it is you, isn't it? You were at the game."

"I think you have me confused with someone else," Brian said.

"See, Kim. C'mon, let's go." Bradley again began to push the chair.

"Brad, I'm fine. It's fine." Kim stepped from the wheelchair and sat beside the man.

"I may sound like a crazy person and my husband might think I am, but lift your shirt sleeve," Kim instructed the hospital patron.

"Kim?!" Brad yelled.

"Brad, trust me. Please lift your sleeve."

"KIM?!"

"Brad, I'm not having this argument with you; not here. Not now. Trust me."

Hesitantly, after five minutes of Kim's non-stop begging and pleading, the man lifted his shirt sleeve as requested. On his upper arm, there it was: the tattoo that he had gotten before he left home, bearing the names of his family members.

"Brian, you came home!" Kim gave him a huge hug. "How did you know we were here?"

"I tried to contact you after the game and they told me you had a family emergency. I slipped on the wet pavement in the parking lot and badly sprained my ankle, so I came here."

"Well, Dad's upstairs, so we need to get up there. Here, you need this wheelchair more than I do." Kim, walking with her husband's arm around her shoulder, pushed her brother to the elevator and headed for Critical Care. When the elevator door opened, Kim could see her family huddled in the hallway, slumped over and crying. Brian, unsure how the rest of the family would react to seeing him, given the circumstances, stayed in the waiting area, as Kim and Bradley ran down the hallway towards the family.

"What happened; what's wrong?" Kim frantically asked.

"He's gone, Kim," her mom said, "Daddy's gone."

"A…third…heart…attack?" Kim asked, choking tears.

"No. He didn't survive the second one. The nurses got a pulse back briefly but it didn't last."

"He didn't see it, did he?" Kim asked in hysterics.

"On the contrary, Kim. I think he saw it from the best seat in the house."

Kim suddenly realized something. Her dad had found Baseball Heaven.

Kim stayed with her mom as Bradley walked to the waiting room to bring Brian to join them.

"C'mon, he's your dad too," Bradley motioned. Brian abruptly realized his hope of rekindling or repairing the fractured friendship with his father was gone. When he reached the family, Brian fell to the floor and loudly wept. Moments later, the remaining Reedeaux family huddled together in a group hug.

A week later, Kim, Brian, and the Reedeaux family buried Harold beside a tall, nearly bare sycamore tree in Pittsburgh's Cascade Memorial Garden. The day before the burial, nearly 2,000 people, including sports figures from three states, fans, former radio co-workers, and the entire Chicago Cubs baseball team, attended Harold's memorial service. As Kim looked around the church during the funeral, she saw so many familiar, influential, and inspiring people in both her father's life and hers. As she analyzed her life, Kim came to a sudden realization: It wasn't her dream she was living; it was her dad's.

In a moment of reflection with "Amazing Grace" filling the sanctuary, Kim recalled a day in 1975 when her dad told his three-year-old little girl about his Big League Dream and how her grandfather called it crazy. In Kim's grandfather's eyes, Harold was a "slow, fat kid from Minne-snow-ta." Harold believed his father and chose sports broadcasting as the "next best thing" to living his Big League dream. Unbeknownst to Kim, that precious memory she had shared with her father, all those years ago, became her first real baseball "moment" and the first strong memory she shared with her dad. After that day, every step she took in her pursuit of baseball had been a tribute to her father, in some form or another.

Harold Reedeaux's life ended before Kim's team won the World Series, but he saw it. If he did not witness the victory from Heaven, he saw it through his daughter's eyes. After all, the "ivy dreams" shared between fathers and daughters are made to last forever.

www.ingramcontent.com/pod-product-compliance
Lightning Source LLC
Chambersburg PA
CBHW020614310726
48979CB00008B/1477/J

* 9 7 8 0 5 7 8 1 1 3 5 3 1 *